ASTROLOGY FOR WITCHES

Astrology for
WITCHES

Enhance Your Rituals, Spells, and
Practices with the Magic of the Cosmos

Michael Herkes

ROCKRIDGE
PRESS

For general information on our other products and services or to obtain technical support, please contact our Customer Care Department within the United States at (866) 744-2665, or outside the United States at (510) 253-0500.

Rockridge Press publishes its books in a variety of electronic and print formats. Some content that appears in print may not be available in electronic books, and vice versa.

Interior and Cover Designer: Mando Daniel
Art Producer: Alyssa Williams
Editor: Brian Sweeting
Production Editor: Ellina Litmanovich
Production Manager: Holly Haydash

Copyright Page: All illustrations used under license from Shutterstock.com

Author Photo courtesy of MRH MultiMedia

Paperback ISBN: 978-1-63878-574-3
eBook ISBN: 978-1-63878-788-4

To Christina Harris—my best friend and soul "sis-star"! Here is to our misty water-colored memories of reading astrology books at Borders over iced coffee and realizing it was the stars that made us this way. I love you and am so happy to share this lifetime with you!

CONTENTS

INTRODUCTION

Hello there.

"What's your sign?"

"What house is your moon in?"

"When were you born?"

I'm sure you've heard these phrases before. I even suspect you may have been caught uttering them yourself, whether in a group of friends gossiping over horoscopes, fishing for compatibility on a date, or filling out an online quiz. While astrology remains a common interest for the masses, it also plays a key role in modern witchcraft. Get a group of witches together, and someone is bound to start asking everyone what their Sun, Moon, and rising signs are in the first few minutes. So, before I go any further, let me introduce myself—my name is Michael, and I am known as the Glam Witch. I love astrology and am an Aries Sun, Libra Moon, with a Virgo rising. Welcome to *Astrology for Witches*, your guide to exploring the magic of the cosmos and manifesting your desires with the power of astrology!

Some of my earliest astrological memories were conversations with my mom as we read over our horoscope in the weekly television listing. This later led to spending hours at local bookstores with my best friend examining compatibility and how our signs make up our personalities. I've always leaned hard into my "sign." It was obvious that I was a full-blooded Aries—full of passion, creativity, and drive, with the patience of a toddler and the shortest temper ever, but that's a fire sign for you! However, that was about the extent of my knowledge.

While I have been practicing witchcraft for more than 20 years, it took me a while to really incorporate astrology into my magic. Everything I picked up on the subject seemed dense, lacking the spark to keep my attention. I felt like astrology as a whole was a puzzle that was missing pieces. Then, several years ago, I had my natal chart read for the first time. I had finally found a translator who could speak to me in a way that I could understand. I started to comprehend the planetary energies and the zodiac in a much more vivid way. Since then, my love and admiration for astrology has magnified, and I have found new and inventive ways to not only use it in my witchcraft for manifestation, but also assist others in understanding their astrological makeup and providing intuitive spiritual guidance. It is my hope that I can pass down this knowledge to you so that you can use the magic of the cosmos to get the most out of your life here on Earth!

HOW TO USE THIS BOOK

This book is a road map for incorporating the stars, planets, and cosmic forces of the universe into your life by way of witchcraft. Whether you are brand-new to astrology and/or witchcraft or have been a practitioner for years, my goal is to present magical and practical ways in which you can use astrology to manifest your desires.

Part 1 of the book provides foundational information on astrology and witchcraft for use in building on the spell-based chapters corresponding to the different planets found in part 2. Each spell chapter includes spells, rituals, or practices that touch on all areas of your life. Exercise patience with yourself as you become comfortable putting what you learn into practice. Astrology can feel daunting at first. Go at your own pace. The exercises will come more easily the more you practice. Focus more on the journey and less on the destination.

Astrology is a tool to unlock your potential on Earth in this lifetime. By understanding how astrology works and your astrological makeup, you can better plan for your future and use the art of magic to manifest your desired destiny. So pack your bags and grab your broomstick as we prepare to launch into the dark abyss of the universe to make some magic!

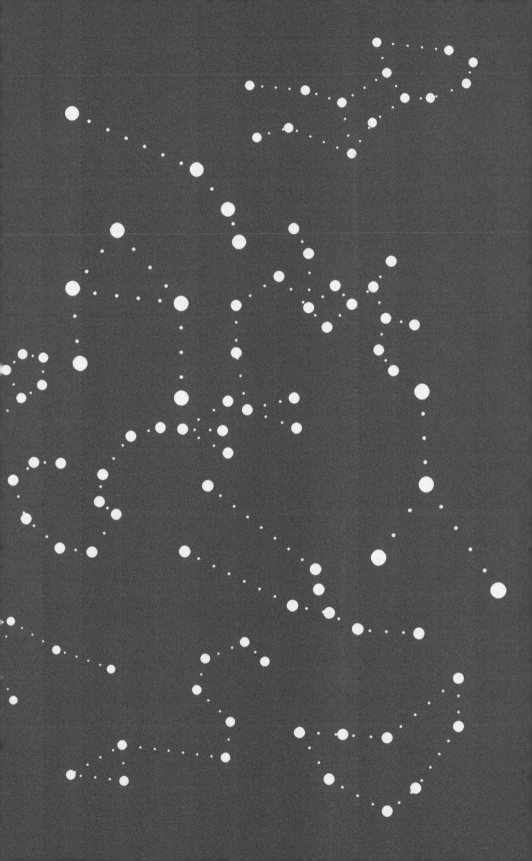

PART I

THE COSMOLOGY OF ASTROLOGY

Welcome to part 1 of *Astrology for Witches*! These chapters provide background information on astrology, including its origins, key elements, and ways it can enhance your life. This information will set the foundation for you to interpret your personal birth chart and create your own horo-scopes. We will also explore the exotic practice of witchcraft and how it can be used in conjunction with astrology for the spells, rituals, and practices outlined in part 2. So, cosmic witch in training, let's dive into the cosmology of astrology!

CHAPTER 1

UNDERSTANDING ASTROLOGY

Thousands of years have passed since people first looked to the sky for guidance and began interpreting the glittering balls of light above to gain insight into their lives. Since then, astrological systems have evolved in new ways as tools for promoting personal growth, predicting events, and becoming attuned to the forces of nature. While reading editorialized horoscopes in periodicals may be entertaining, it is but a small piece of astrology and its use in daily life today. This chapter will provide an overview of what astrology is, what it is not, its historical relevance, and ways in which it can empower your life.

WHAT IS ASTROLOGY?

Everything in the universe is connected, and as we live our lives on a day-to-day basis, we are influenced by the cosmos. This is most notably seen concerning the seasonal shifts governed by the Sun and the Moon's gravitational influence. However, each heavenly body is a source of energy that ultimately contributes to our lives. Astrology began as a cosmic language that helped provide meaning for life's paradoxes and explained natural agricultural and meteorological events as they took place on Earth. However, it expanded over time as astrologers began to see and define the inextricable link between the planets and our daily routines.

Simply put, astrology uses the different star systems, luminaries, and planets to make distinctions about people's personality and character, in addition to how the celestial movements influence their lives here on Earth. This is done by mathematically calculating the positions of the different planets at the time of birth and the interpretation of their continued movements through the solar system. Astrology has been considered a scholarly tradition for most of its history and has influenced many scholarly disciplines, including astronomy, alchemy, meteorology, psychology, medicine, and the occult. Consequently, those who study astrology are considered astrologers, and there are many different branches and schools of thought in the field.

ASTROLOGICAL MISNOMERS

Understanding precisely what astrology *is* can be easier when we examine what it *isn't*. Astrology is not a science. Research has found no conclusive evidence that planetary alignments affect our lives. However, it was never intended to be a science. Instead, like religion, astrology can be used in a healthy, nondogmatic way to give spiritual significance to life's patterns and stimulate thought. It is, however, a detailed math-based form of divination that can help anchor your life and provide insight into your personality while empowering you to create your best individual destiny.

Astrology is not silly entertainment. Unfortunately, many people believe that astrology is made up and that the traits of each sign can be applied to everyone. But in fact, this latter point is correct, and it is the entire point. While astrology shows our individual characteristics, it also reveals universal patterns that can be used to understand aspects of our life better, making it a valuable tool for spiritual growth and mental health.

While astrology can certainly be coupled with other metaphysical techniques, such as reading tarot cards or tea leaves, mediumship, numerology, and palmistry, astrology is distinct from these. Astrology is also not the same thing as being intuitive or psychic. Instead, it is a logical practice.

Astrology is not going to solve all your problems. In using astrology to decode our personalities and foresee the future, it is essential to understand that it alone will never solve all your concerns, nor will every horoscope be 100 percent true for you.

THE ORIGINS OF ASTROLOGY

Astrological principles have been used by Indigenous people around the world as relevant to their local star systems and cultural beliefs. Its origins can be traced back to ancient Mesopotamia around 3000 BCE. There, stargazers searched for meaning in the sky and identified various constellations, along with five "wandering" stars that, when combined with the Sun and Moon, became the seven classical planets of antiquity. Between the 19th and 17th centuries BCE, the Babylonians developed the concept of the zodiac by observing the apparent path of the Sun and planets as they moved across the sky. The zodiac was measured into 12 equal segments and named after neighboring constellations that were linked to various deities. As a result, the varying positions they observed were considered to be divinely influential. By the 16th century BCE, the Babylonians had begun to use astrology as an omen-based practice.

But the Babylonians were not alone in their study of the sky. Vedic, or Jyotish, astrology appeared in Indian texts dating back to around 1400 BCE; however, it is speculated that it may have originated between 10,000 and 5000 BCE. Chinese astrology appeared during the Zhou dynasty, around 1046 BCE.

By the first century BCE, Babylonian astrological practices moved to the Eastern Mediterranean, where they became popular in Egypt and were later advanced by the Greeks. The first evidence of astrological charts being used is around this time. Astrological concepts would eventually travel to central and western Europe, where the ancient practices were advanced further by medieval astrologers. As interest in astrological study and practice grew, it was eventually linked to mathematics and medicine in the Middle Ages. Because of the dominance of the Catholic Church and later the beliefs associated with the Age of Enlightenment, interest in astrological principles waned in Europe from the 17th century until the later part of the 19th century.

THE BIRTH OF CONTEMPORARY ASTROLOGY

A revival of interest in astrology was stimulated by the work of William Frederick Allan in the 19th century. Altering his name to Alan Leo based on his zodiac sign, Leo is generally referred to as "the father of contemporary astrology," and with good reason. He set out to rebrand the traditional astrology of his time into something that moved beyond its initial concepts. After becoming a member of the Theosophical Society in 1890, Leo started developing a more spiritual and psychological foundation for astrology that focused on character analysis. He also advocated for a broader interpretation of event prediction than previous astrologers, who focused almost entirely on precise prophecy and foresight. This approach led to the use of Sun-sign astrology and the production of horoscope columns.

"Humanistic" astrology was introduced by Dane Rudhyar, another influential modern astrologer. Largely influenced by the writings of Carl G. Jung, Rudhyar's astrological approach focused on the internal forces that make us human and popularized astrology in the new age movement of the 1970s.

DIFFERENT SCHOOLS & BRANCHES OF ASTROLOGY

There are many different schools of astrology, each with their own unique system that illustrates our connection to the cosmos. Following is a small snapshot of some of these different systems and how they differ in practice.

EVOLUTIONARY ASTROLOGY uses the concept of reincarnation when reading a birth chart to track the soul's journey through multiple lifetimes. It considers the lessons from past lives and how souls move to the next, ultimately conspiring in our cosmic spiritual destiny.

PSYCHOLOGICAL ASTROLOGY uses astrology as a tool for reflection on the psyche and how people operate from a psychological perspective. It uses the planets in the natal chart to explain how we act, communicate, feel, and relate to external stimuli.

TRADITIONAL ASTROLOGY uses key concepts from the astrological practices developed between 400 BCE and 1700 CE, including Hellenistic, medieval, and Renaissance astrology. One of these concepts is the use of the natal chart as a defining factor for all aspects of your external life versus your internal psyche. They also do not include Uranus, Neptune, Pluto, or any asteroids in the practice.

VEDIC ASTROLOGY is a traditional Hindu system of astrology that is most frequently practiced in India. It uses the sidereal zodiac, not the tropical zodiac used in Western astrology. The difference is that sidereal astrology uses the real location of planets at the

→

time of birth instead of taking a seasonal approach. In other words, while Western astrology uses a zodiac based on the seasons, Vedic astrology is based on the actual constellations in the sky. Vedic astrology is more religious and connected to Hinduism. Vedic astrology will not be covered in this book.

In addition to these schools, there are different branches of astrology that discuss how astrological concepts can be applied to various things. These include:

ELECTIONAL ASTROLOGY is a system used to determine when an event should take place. It is a form of predictive astrology used to determine when to do something.

FINANCIAL ASTROLOGY refers to the use of astrology to understand and study cosmic movements in connection to the economic market and financial theory.

HORARY ASTROLOGY is a system in which the answers to questions are determined based on the exact time the question is asked.

LOVE ASTROLOGY examines the relationship compatibility between individuals. This can be done through synastry or composite charts. Synastry is a close comparison of the relationships between two distinct natal charts. A composite chart, on the other hand, is the creation of a new "partnership" chart of the midpoints between two individual charts.

MEDICAL ASTROLOGY is a system of astrology used to interpret and understand body parts, illnesses, and medical treatments.

HOW ASTROLOGY CAN HELP YOU

On a very basic level, we all want to live life more comfortably, whether that's by relocating to a place that offers more opportunity, purchasing a car to travel, or changing careers to pursue passions and earn more money. In the same way, astrology can be seen as a useful tool to make navigating life easier by providing insights.

PROVIDE DIRECTION & PURPOSE IN LIFE

When you examine what is written in the stars, you have a better chance of understanding your direction and purpose. Your birth chart is essentially the compass of your life. While it is not necessarily a finite illustration of your destiny, it is a blueprint for personal self-discovery. Using your birth chart will help you in creating self-awareness and lead to introspective moments during which you can realign your focus and purpose. By providing a deeper understanding of who you are and why you do the things you do, astrology can help you better understand yourself and others.

IMPROVE MENTAL HEALTH & SELF-CARE

Astrology can provide a sense of order during times of chaos. Self-care is the process of putting your personal needs first and identifying solutions that leave you feeling fulfilled. Understanding the traits of each sign within your chart can highlight challenges and offer specific ways to implement self-care practices, ultimately realigning the mind, body, and spirit.

ENHANCE CONNECTION TO SPIRITUALITY

Not only can astrology help people better understand their personality, but it can also guide them through various areas of life, including spiritual development. Attuning to spirituality with astrology will allow for you to divine your life with unbridled creativity and inspiration, as well as create a moral and ethical way to move through your life.

PREPARE FOR THE FUTURE

Perhaps the best-known practice in astrology is the use of horoscopes. Horoscopes have become a fun and trendy way to identify themes in your life based on the forces of the universe. These forecasts use the zodiac sign the Sun was in at the time of birth and how the various planets and other objects in space move over time. Using horoscopes in astrology can help people better prepare for what is coming and navigate life, although it does not control fate.

CREATE CHANGE FOR FAVORABLE OUTCOMES

Astrology offers only a forecast, much like a weatherperson who is reading high- and low-pressure systems and making hypotheses. It will not necessarily rain each time they predict rain. However, by knowing the probable chances based on the supporting data, you can better prepare, such as by grabbing an umbrella. We all have free will to change course and affect the situations at hand. For example, you don't have to have a challenging day at work simply because a horoscope predicts a difficult day. You can make necessary changes to your daily routines or behaviors, such as working slowly to avoid mistakes and communicating with care.

THE ASTROLOGICAL BASICS

There are many components to astrology, but don't get overwhelmed! This is a brief introduction to the key tenets of astrology: the modalities, elements, signs, planets, and houses—all of which we will explore at greater length in chapter 3.

MODALITIES

The three modalities in astrology are key to understanding how different personalities express energy and respond to action. The modalities are made up of cardinal signs, fixed signs, and mutable signs. Each of the four elements contains these three modalities, with each modality also being attributed to four zodiac signs. In short, the modalities identify those who are assertive and bold, those who are practical and stubborn, and those who are adaptable and go with the flow.

ELEMENTS

Astrology uses the four classical elements of fire, earth, air, and water to further distinguish energetic themes of the zodiac signs. Each element has its own set of qualities connected to the corresponding elements. For example, fire signs are warm and transformative; earth signs are grounded and nurturing; air signs are whimsical and adaptable; and water signs are deep and fluid. Each of the four elements rules over three signs, and they further describe the actions of the signs.

ZODIAC SIGNS

The zodiac is an imaginary band that follows the ecliptic around Earth, and it overlaps with 13 constellations. It is divided into 12 equal 30° segments. Each sign poses a unique set of traits illustrating strengths, weaknesses, and personalities reflecting an individual's way of life. The zodiac is divided into 12 sections, with counterclockwise motion that is east of the vernal equinox. The zodiac signs are Aries, Taurus, Gemini, Cancer, Leo, Virgo, Libra, Scorpio, Sagittarius, Capricorn, Aquarius, and Pisces.

PLANETS

When our ancestors observed the night sky, they not only saw the stars, but also the planets. Classical astrology used the Sun, Moon, Mercury, Venus, Mars, Jupiter, and Saturn as the astrological planets. These planets were associated with various gods, and each god's corresponding rulership was applied to a planet. Modern astrology has expanded on this by incorporating Uranus, Neptune, and Pluto. As each planet orbits the Sun, it spends time in each sign of the zodiac. Each zodiac sign is governed by a planetary force, which provides a snapshot into unconscious needs and desires. Much of a sign's makeup stems from the energy associated with a specific planet.

HOUSES

The houses in astrology help define different areas of life, starting with the self, moving into society, and ultimately culminating in the collective unconscious. The houses planets are located in at the time of birth provide the big picture regarding what areas of life will matter most for that individual. Likewise, as the planets transit in various houses, they can point to shifting influences and where attention should be placed.

KEY TAKEAWAYS

Now that you have been introduced to what astrology is and is not and how it can help your life, here are some key takeaways to keep in mind as we move into the next chapter and explore the practice of witchcraft and how it connects to astrology.

- **Astrology is an ancient practice.** Dating back to the Babylonians, cultures around the world have looked to the sky for meaning and for divine understanding.

- **Astrology is more than a silly pastime.** It has been used for centuries to provide meaning and personal empowerment.

- **Astrology can help many parts of life.** Studying the planetary motions can offer purpose and direction, understanding of the self, spiritual connection, and assistance in overcoming obstacles.

- **Astrology is not fated.** You have freedom of will to make changes. Use astrology as a forecast to plan accordingly for your desired outcomes.

CHAPTER 2

WITCHCRAFT & ASTROLOGY

Modern witchcraft stems from pre-Christian pagan practices of the ancient world. However, today a witch may be that coworker with the desk covered in crystals, the woman in the grocery store with a basket full of fresh flowers and spices, or the man walking down the street with his gaze fixated on the sky. Witches are everywhere. But what exactly *is* a witch? And what does being one have to do with astrology? This chapter will explore these questions and illustrate how the practices of witchcraft and astrology intersect.

THE PRACTICE OF WITCHCRAFT

Witchcraft has long been shrouded in mystery and superstition. Today, many people are reclaiming the title of "witch" and conjuring spells and rituals adapted from centuries of magical and occult practices. For years, as a result of religious propaganda, being labeled a witch could get you killed, such as during the European witch hunts of the Middle Ages and the Salem witch trials in colonial Massachusetts. However, as witches began to come out of the broom closet in the 1960s and '70s, the public began to learn that witches were not in league with the Christian concept of the devil.

In Hollywood, the witch has been treated as fantastical with special effects and supernatural conjurations, like in *Charmed*, *The Craft*, and *American Horror Story: Coven*. But that is the biggest misconception in Hollywood—that witchcraft is fantasy or make-believe. In reality, modern witchcraft is a bona fide spiritual path.

A witch is any person who taps into and manipulates energy to change their life and the world around them. Everything in the world is made up of energy, and witches couple their intentions with the forces of nature to achieve manifestations. The practice of witchcraft enhances practitioners' connection to life. Being a witch means focusing less on what is physically visible and more on what is beyond our vision, in the form of synchronicity, signs, and unexplainable connections. The practice of witchcraft entails using intuition to create the life you want.

HOW SPELLS WORK

A witch's spell is like a prayer, and there are many different ways to craft a spell. In general, it starts with an intention, which is coupled with ingredients that align with your goals and then executed in ritualistic practice. It can be very easy for someone to tell you how you *should* practice. However, your spellcraft can be as simple or complex as you wish. Much of the magic I perform is conjured up in my mind. However, different ingredients can amplify intentions. When I am in the mood for more ceremonial rituals, I perform candle-based spells. If I am doing a healing spell, I often make magical baths. Sometimes,

I light certain candles, blend incense by crushing herbs, or mix magical oils as part of my spellcraft. Or I may wear a certain color daily to align with the energy I am trying to manipulate in my favor. In general, my practice is solitary, although I will occasionally do a simple spell with friends over brunch—toasting our magical mimosas while empowering each other with successful endeavors. In this case, oranges radiate the energy of abundance and success, while champagne is used for celebration. Mixing the two ingredients with intentions, speaking words of affirmation, and visualizing a goal is a form of spellcraft, just as making a wish and blowing out a birthday candle is one. Regardless of what type of spell I am doing, during the spell I consider what I want to accomplish and visualize it taking shape, and then use practical means to achieve it in real life.

THE CONNECTION BETWEEN WITCHCRAFT & ASTROLOGY

Both witchcraft and astrology have been used in unison for centuries. In ancient times, the planets were deemed gods who created Earth and governed over certain areas of life. Meanwhile, priests and priestesses were appointed to execute various rituals to honor and commune with the celestial bodies. These rituals often included ceremonial sacrifices and other offerings to bless the land and people. They would also read the stars to help predict the future. Many modern witchcraft practices incorporate elements of astrology in celebration, worship, spellcasting, and divination. The more a witch understands astrological forces, the more they will be able to connect the dots to other aspects of the craft.

HOW IS ASTROLOGY USED IN WITCHCRAFT?

While astrology and witchcraft remain two separate practices, witches use astrology in their spells and rituals, sometimes even without knowing it. Witchcraft is saturated with symbolism, and many astrological correspondences are often applied to areas of magic and spellcraft today. This may be by way of strengthening a connection to the natural world, deciding magical timing, choosing certain divination practices, and enhancing spellcraft with astrologically aligned ingredients.

BOND WITH THE NATURAL WORLD

Witchcraft is deeply connected to nature, honoring all aspects of it as sacred. My dear friend and fellow witch author Fiona Horne has said that "nature is the witch's bible." It is constantly teaching us if we listen and look. Astrology is another way for witches to elevate their practices and sync their energies to the movement of the universe. Over time, certain plants were found to both heal and harm. The physical and medicinal elements of plants are also used energetically in magic. Plants later became interrelated with astrology. Similarly, crystals have become associated with specific planets. Witches celebrate the seasonal Sun festivals known as Sabbats and Moon rituals called Esbats, aligning with the cosmic forces and their connection to Earth. Everything within our universe is nature, including the planets, moons, stars, and all bodies in the cosmos.

MAGICAL TIMING

One of the biggest ways astrology is used in witchcraft is through magical timing. Many witches use the astrological energies of the different Moon phases to enhance their magic. The different hours of the day, days of the week, seasons, etc., all correspond to different planets and zodiac signs that can further assist in magic. By knowing the power of timing, witches can make informed decisions about their spellcraft and determine the best time to maximize manifestations.

DIVINATORY DEALINGS

Divination is the magical art of foreseeing the future. Predictive astrology uses astrological transits to create horoscopes. This is a form of divination. Additionally, astrology is an underlying current in the divinatory practices of tarot and palmistry. The standard modern tarot deck is 78 cards, and all align with a different zodiac sign to bring additional foresight to readings. They can also be used in conjunction with horoscopes to look deeper into potential outcomes. Witches often do tarot readings during specific phases of the Moon or astrological events. Similarly, palmistry uses the shape, lines, and aspects of our hands to further explore personality and predict the future. For example, different shapes and sizes of the hand are attributed to the elements, and planetary influence is found in areas of the palm, with three signs considered to be housed in each finger.

PERSONALIZE YOUR RITUALS

A witch's magic lies in the spells, rituals, and practices they perform to create desired change. To do this, witches use a variety of ingredients aligned with their intention. Elements of astrology can be incorporated into magical practices by examining the various correspondences that interact with a witch's personal birth chart. For example, you might wish to carry a crystal that corresponds to each of your astrological signs or carve a combination of your planetary symbols into the wax of a candle for enchantment. Astrology opens another door to personalizing your witchcrafting.

THE BENEFITS OF ASTROLOGY FOR A WITCH

The only constant in life is change, and witchcraft is deeply connected to the art of transformation. It can be very easy to get complacent and stagnant in your practice. There are several niche areas of magic that witches may choose to explore or bring into their practice. Each can have a dramatic effect on their ability to manifest. So, taking yourself out of your comfort zone to continue learning will only help you evolve in your magical practice.

UNDERSTAND YOUR INNER NATURE

Nature goes far beyond the earthly elements, climate, plants, and animals. It is also our inner emotional landscape and the universe we inhabit. For this reason, astrology can be seen not only as a blueprint for unlocking your inner magic but also as a means to maximize your potential. Taking time for introspection and reflection is one way witches can develop a sense of empowerment. Astrology helps you dig deeper into who you are and honor the magic of you, beam with big witch energy, and shine brighter while attracting good fortune.

FORECASTING YOUR FUTURE

The movement of the celestial forces can be precalculated, resulting in an energetic forecast of what's to come. This is done by examining astrological transits in connection to a birth chart with the ongoing movement of planets on their orbital paths through the cosmos. As planets travel through the different zodiac signs, houses, and angles created by the proximity between planets, the cosmic forces can be used to forecast your life. By understanding what is coming, you can make the best decisions for yourself. Planetary returns (when a planet is in the same position it was at the time of your birth) are one such forecast used to prepare for clean slates and fresh starts.

OVERCOME CHALLENGES

In the same way that astrology can help predict the future, it can also help you overcome obstacles. One way is by providing insight into why you are the way you are. This is a useful means of healing yourself and reinvigorating your life with self-acceptance and self-compassion. Astrological study, symbolism, and magic can all provide additional ambition and motivation to move through hard times. Remember that everything is built on cycles. Our seasons shift and change, the moon passes through phases from complete darkness to light, and orbiting planets will eventually move beyond their current positions.

COMPATIBILITY IN YOUR RELATIONSHIPS

If you have ever filled out an online dating profile, chances are you've been asked what your sign is. Astrological influences can identify key components of our personality and emotional landscape. This can help determine your cosmic compatibility with others. This is one reason why magazines, blogs, and apps note that certain zodiac signs are more harmonious matches than others. Witches can thus use their birth charts to call forth the perfect love with a "come to me" love spell. However, compatibility-based astrology is not limited to finding a perfect match. You can also examine how your natal chart corresponds with those of others in your life (e.g., people with whom you have a romantic, platonic, familial, or professional connection) and use magic to work through indifference and maximize harmony.

STEPS FOR INCORPORATING ASTROLOGY INTO YOUR CRAFT

Starting any new practice can be daunting, especially when the subject matter is as broad and detailed as astrology. It would probably take a lifetime or two to truly master the art of astrological study and magic. However, the beauty is in the journey. As you step further along your path of incorporating astrology into your magical practice, consider the following tips.

SUSPEND CYNICISM & DISBELIEF

Avoid becoming overwhelmed by going easy on yourself and having faith in your magic. The most important part to starting anything is having an open mind. As you progress in your studies and practice, remain open to experimentation. This will help you develop a greater awareness of your own practice and release you from any self-sabotaging judgment. Any new practice takes time and energy before it fully clicks. So, take a deep breath and relax. Allow yourself to believe in the infinite possibilities of the universe.

DEVOTE TIME TO LEARNING

Simply showing up for your practice and yourself is a pivotal step. However, it can be easy to hit a plateau. Make the effort to challenge yourself to try different things along the way. Experiment and watch how your life unfolds as a result. When we are out of our comfort zone, true growth blossoms. The best way to incorporate astrology into your craft is to commit to studying it. Much of Hollywood witchcraft is "instant," but in reality, persistence is critical. Supplement the knowledge you gain here with additional books, online courses, and other resources available to you. I share some of my recommendations for further study on page 174.

START WITH YOUR INTERESTS

Even though spellcasting and ritual are serious ways to manifest your desires, I am a firm believer that you should have fun doing it. Your astrological magic should be rewarding and have a positive effect on your growth and development. Make note of what you are drawn to in both witchcraft and astrology. What speaks to you? Why? What do you find most challenging? Why? Keep these questions in mind as you progress and see if there are astrological correspondences at play that might affect your answers.

STAY TAPPED IN

Even though we do not feel the Earth's orbit, we are constantly in motion. Maximize your astrological and planetary magic by staying tapped into the transits of relevant cosmic bodies and how they affect your natal chart. Transits will have a direct impact on your natal chart. By tracking them, you can start to formulate your own horoscopes and better prepare for the future. Download the apps, supplement your readings with books that map out future transits, and use calendars that provide astrological data to accomplish this.

SET INTENTIONS & ACT ACCORDINGLY

Having a clear vision in mind is vital when deciding what you wish to accomplish with your spellcraft. Your intention is just one of the ingredients needed for successful spellcasting. Your intentions should be anchored in passion. When you anchor your goals in something that you truly believe in and feel passionate about, you have a good chance for success. However, manifesting doesn't stop with intentions. You must also follow up your magical efforts with real-life action. Astrology helps in assessing when and how to follow up your spellcraft with practical application.

BE PATIENT & ADAPTABLE

When casting a spell, you can't possibly foresee all the possible outcomes it may have. It's critical to account for this. Likewise, the universe does not adhere to our understanding of time. Some spells will take longer to manifest than others. Sometimes, the celestial forces have better things in store for us. The universe has a lot of say. Avoid micromanaging results or constantly questioning when your intentions will manifest. For instance, let's say you've done a spell to land a job you've always wanted. After working the spell and doing the physical real-life work to get hired, you are rejected. You may think the spell didn't work until a few weeks later, when you receive a lead to another job that sounds even better and you land it. You would not have applied had you gotten the first job. So do not get discouraged if your spells are seemingly not working. Instead, consider what the universe may be saying to you and move in that direction.

KEY TAKEAWAYS

So now you know a bit about how modern witchcraft can use astrology to enhance magical practice. Following are some key takeaways to keep in mind as we move into the next chapter and explore the various components that make up astrology.

- **Witchcraft is a form of empowerment.** Unlike the Hollywood glitz and glamour of special-effects witchcraft or mainstream society's misconception that witches are inherently evil, witchcraft is a spiritual practice used to manifest desired changes and forge personal empowerment.

- **Spells are a witch's prayer.** Starting first with an intention, infused with corresponding energetically chosen components, and later followed up with real-life action, spells are powerful tools for manifestation. There are many different ways to cast a spell, and astrology can influence it in a number of ways.

- **Astrology can elevate a witch's craft.** From being a powerful tool for introspection, form of divination, aspect of timing, resource for relationships, and means for overcoming obstacles, witches will benefit from incorporating astrology into their path.

- **Devote time to learning.** The only way to successfully apply astrology to your path is to devote time to learning. Reading this book now is a powerful first step, and I know you will continue to prosper in your studies and application.

CHAPTER 3

YOUR CONNECTION
TO THE COSMOS

Before you can start reading your natal chart,
you first must understand all the components it
will include. Let's start by building a foundation
for interpreting your astrological portrait. In this
chapter, you are going to learn about the various
modalities, elements, zodiac signs, planets, and
houses that are in astrology to better understand
your connection to the cosmos.

THE MODALITIES

The modalities are cardinal, fixed, and mutable. Each of the four elements are found in one of the modalities. This is called "quadru- plicities." The combined quality of each element and modality show how various personalities express energy and respond to action. A sign's modality is also connected to each sign's seasonal place- ment. Because the sign Aries appears in the first month of spring in the Western Hemisphere, it's a cardinal sign. The signs' individ- ual characteristics are determined by the combination of element and modality. Aries, in this instance, is the cardinal fire sign, which creates an association with action (cardinal modality) in creative passion (fire element).

CARDINAL

The cardinal signs are Aries, Cancer, Libra, and Capricorn. Cardinal energy is raw, creative, and new. Each cardinal sign marks the begin- ning of a new season, further illustrating the sense of freshness with which these signs come. Cardinals are the initiators and self-starters of the modalities and often considered very independent. They come with a mission to move ahead and love to take charge. They want nothing more than to win, and are seen as leaders, trendsetters, and trailblazers.

FIXED

The fixed signs are Taurus, Leo, Scorpio, and Aquarius. Fixed signs are the midpoint of each seasonal energy and place emphasis on sustainability, preservation, and maintaining the energy of their sign. They are stable, independent, and reliable. However, being fixed means that they are not prone to movement. They are slow and methodical and can be extremely stubborn. Fixed signs thrive in the areas of routine and perfection, making them instrumental when it comes to getting things done right.

MUTABLE

The mutable signs are Gemini, Virgo, Sagittarius, and Pisces. Mutable signs mark transition. They are focused on adapting for the change of the next season, picking up the pieces of the other modalities in their season, and shifting in a new direction to ensure survival. As the chameleon of the modalities, this makes them flexible and able to see life through varied perspectives, showcasing a high level of intelligence. They are quick to think on their feet and be resourceful. However, while embracing their versatility, they can often be contradictory. On the bright side, they always know how to bounce back.

THE ELEMENTS

You may have come across terms like "fire sign" or "water sign" while reading horoscopes or engaging in conversations about astrology. This is because the 12 zodiac signs are divided into the four elements of fire, earth, air, and water. Each element is paired with three signs—each of a different modality. Not surprisingly, witchcraft and other occult practices also use these elements to better understand energetic qualities. Some examples would be the elemental links to the suits of tarot cards or calling upon the elements in structured ritual formats by casting a circle. Knowing which element governs your sign helps you gain a better understanding of your own inner nature, while also illustrating compatibility. Earth and water signs are more harmoniously paired than fire and air. Understanding the elements gives you a better sense of how each element works from an energetic standpoint.

FIRE △

The fire signs are Aries, Leo, and Sagittarius, ruling the first, fifth, and ninth houses of astrology. Fire is a constantly moving element, so it comes as no surprise that fire signs are full of energy, ambition, and drive. They are motivated by action and creativity. Just as a flame provides warmth, fire signs are known for having over-the-top personalities that blanket situations with fun and exuberance. On the flip side, this can sometimes burn out of control with ego, bossiness, and hot tempers. Overall, though, when fire signs appear in a natal chart, they represent an area in your life that is full of creative passion and enthusiasm. Channel the element of fire to radiate courage, strength, and leadership.

EARTH ▽

The earth signs are Taurus, Virgo, and Capricorn. The element also rules over the second, sixth, and tenth houses of astrology. Earth signs are grounded and more practical than passionate. They seek pleasure in routine and structure, which can make them stubborn. Earth is also sensualistic, with a fond love of food, wine, art, and other worldly possessions. Therefore, earth signs can be materialistic. Due to their practicality, they are often associated with amassing wealth. They are also deeply connected to aspects of physical nature. Earth signs in a person's natal chart often denote realistic responsibility and dependability. Work with earth's elemental aspects of astrology to create stability in routines, maximize loyalty, and build foundations.

AIR △

The air signs are Gemini, Libra, and Aquarius. Air also rules the third, seventh, and eleventh houses of astrology. These signs are linked to the power of intellect, imagination, and communication. They are also highly adaptable in social situations, making them friendly and charismatic individuals. When air signs appear in a natal chart, they represent charm and communicativeness, with curiosity for innovation. However, air energy can sometimes be flaky, fickle, and can manifest as being a bit of an *air*head. Because air-sign Suns are very cerebral and always thinking, they may also appear cold or detached, as they are more logical than emotional. Call upon the element of air when seeking mental stimulation or clarity or help with communication.

WATER △

The water signs are Cancer, Scorpio, and Pisces, which rule the fourth, eighth, and twelfth houses of astrology. Whether calm like a placid lake or as destructive as a tidal wave, water signs have intense emotions. This allows them to have deep empathy and compassion for others. However, the flip side is that their emotions can take over and hit them like a tsunami. Known for having a keen sense of instinct, water signs are very observant and trust their intuition. However, this can sometimes cause them to overthink things. Water signs are also known for being as deep as the ocean floor, interested in powerful emotional conversations that stimulate their vivid imaginations. The areas where water signs appear in your chart denote emotion, sensitivity, and empathy. Call upon the element of water to cool your soul, get in touch with your emotions, or balance your feelings.

THE ZODIAC SIGNS

The Earth orbits around the Sun, but from our view on Earth, it appears to be the opposite. The ecliptic is the apparent path of the Sun around the Earth. The sun sets the line of the ecliptic, and all the planets (except for Pluto) follow this same path. The zodiac is the imaginary band that follows the ecliptic around Earth, and it overlaps with 13 constellations, which are divided into 12 parts, in 30° sections. The zodiac signs travel in a counterclockwise direction east of the vernal equinox in the following order: Aries, Taurus, Gemini, Cancer, Leo, Virgo, Libra, Scorpio, Sagittarius, Capricorn, Aquarius, and Pisces.

These signs each have their own set of characteristics that describe ways of life, such as strengths, weaknesses, and personalities, for those born under them. Each sign is also linked to mythologies, colors, minerals, and bodily rulers, among other things. Understanding their indications helps paint the picture of who you are.

ARIES

Date Range: March 21–April 19

Element: fire

Ruling Planet: Mars

Modality: cardinal

Symbol: the ram

Best Qualities: adventurous, ambitious, driven, and optimistic

Challenging Qualities: controlling, impatient, insensitive, and short-tempered

Body Rulership: head, brain, face, and eyes

Mantra: "I am."

Crystals: amethyst, aquamarine, bloodstone, diamond, garnet, and pyrite

Color: rich warm tones of red, orange, yellow, and hot pinks

Those born under the very fiery and feisty sign of Aries are headstrong and independent, making this a sign of action. This sign's season starts with the spring equinox, bringing bold and vivacious energy. Individuals with Aries placements in their chart will possess energy and determination. Aries likes to take the lead and be in control. Being the first of the signs makes Aries the "baby" of the zodiac, resulting in a tendency for knee-jerk reactions and temper tantrums. Ruled by Mars, the god of war, Aries is a trigger-happy warrior that can rush recklessly into battle. However, this fighter mentality lends it ambition and confidence. Aries is connected to identity and asks us to consider, "Who am I" and "What do I want?" For this reason, it is a great sign to help tap into your desires to push past boundaries, gain confidence, and be assertive. Aries energy has no time for patience or anything that is "slow." This sign wants it all, and it wants it now. Therefore, it is a wonderful energy to use for new beginnings and starting projects. Being that it is such an active sign, it can also stimulate physical vigor and stagnant energy.

TAURUS

Date Range: April 20–May 20

Element: earth

Ruling Planet: Venus

Modality: fixed

Symbol: the bull

Best Qualities: loving and patient

Challenging Qualities: lazy, materialistic, possessive, and stubborn

Body Rulership: neck, throat, mouth, and thyroid

Mantra: "I have."

Crystals: aventurine, amber, emerald, lapis, rhodonite, and rose quartz

Colors: shades of green, brown, light pinks, and pastels

Taurus is a very grounded sign that loves feelings of comfort and beauty. Taurus season takes place during mid-spring, a time when flowers are blooming and the world is invigorated with lushness. It's no surprise then that this sign's element is earth, and individuals connected to this sign have a deep appreciation of nature and the aesthetic. When Taurus appears in a natal chart, it will draw upon the sign's need and love for comfort and things that bring physical and emotional joy, such as food, sex, and luxury items. Taurean placements will also have a need for routine and dislike sudden or forced change. They are represented by the bull, after all, and poking a bull is ill advised. Being ruled by Venus, the goddess of love, Taurus is sensual and deeply connected to the senses. However, they are often considered lazy or possessive. Taurus energy asks us to consider, "What do I have?" and reexamine it as "What do I need?" to find comfort. For this reason, it can be a great energetic anchor for stability or routine.

GEMINI

Date Range: May 21–June 21

Element: air

Ruling Planet: Mercury

Modality: mutable

Symbol: the twins

Best Qualities: adaptability, creativity, imagination, and open-mindedness

Challenging Qualities: anxiety, irritability, gossiping, and two-facedness

Body Rulership: arms, shoulders, hands, lungs, and nervous system

Mantra: "I think."

Crystals: agate, apophyllite, celestite, citrine, opal, and tiger's eye

Colors: shades of yellow, blues, and grays

Gemini dominates all aspects of communication and mental prowess. This is a very expressive sign, and it makes for talented artists who can convey meaning through any medium. Ruled by the "twins," Geminis are known for having a fun, youthful, and playful personality. This also allows them to see both sides of a situation in a logical way, illustrating their flexibility. However, their two-sidedness can also make them seem to flip-flop. This sign excels in intellectual realms. They make for excellent teachers and mentors. However, they also have the ability to detach quickly and bounce to new ideas or thoughts that are more interesting. Because their mind is always turned on, Geminis have a tendency to be very anxious or high strung. Gemini placements put an emphasis on verbal connection, with a witty and flexible approach to new ideas. They ask us to consider how to communicate and express our needs.

CANCER

Date Range: June 21–July 22

Element: water

Ruling Planet: Moon

Modality: cardinal

Symbol: the crab

Best Qualities: compassionate, helpful, intuitive, and loving

Challenging Qualities: clingy, insecure, moody, and suspicious

Body Rulership: chest/breast and stomach

Mantra: "I feel."

Crystals: moonstone, ocean jasper, opal, pearl, and selenite

Colors: shades of blue, purple, and turquoise, sandy tones, white, and black

Cancer is a sensitive water sign that envelops life with love and nurturing. Those born under this sign are known for being highly receptive to their emotions and for having empathy. This sign craves security and, like the crab, finds comfort being in its own shell. Therefore, despite their nurturing nature, Cancers can sometimes come off as cold and suspicious. They often have trouble communicating verbally because when they do, they come across as clingy or insecure. However, despite their sensitive nature, Cancers are known to have a good sense of humor and seek joy from laughter and feel-good vibes. As a cardinal sign, Cancers can initiate new projects in highly imaginative and artistic ways. Cancerian placements in your chart showcase areas of your life in which you are particularly intuitive and sensitive. They ask us to explore our emotional landscapes and listen to the instinctive nature of our feelings.

LEO

Date Range: July 23–August 22

Element: fire

Ruling Planet: Sun

Modality: fixed

Symbol: the lion

Best Qualities: charismatic, confident, loyal, and warm

Challenging Qualities: demanding, dramatic, egotistical, and self-centered

Body Rulership: heart, spine, and upper back

Mantra: "I will."

Crystals: amber, citrine, peridot, ruby, sunstone, and tiger's eye

Colors: warm yellow, orange, and gold, and bold neon shades

Leos are the superstar of the signs. Just like the lion, Leos are courageous, strong, and confident. They have a flair for all things dramatic and exude a passionate independence. Nevertheless, like their ruling planet the Sun, they shine with a warmth that draws others to their magnetic personalities. They excel when they are the center of attention. As a result, they can be vain and egotistical. This comes from Leos' longing to feel valued and appreciated. Leos have a huge heart and are very generous. They are wildly loyal to those they care about and are motivated by their responsibilities. Leos have an energetic dichotomy to them, since theirs is a fixed fire sign. Fire moves but the fixed modality does not. Therefore, the best explanation of Leos is that of a fireplace—a contained flame. Leo placements illuminate areas where you take center stage. This sign asks us to examine what it is we want and manifest it into being with pure confidence.

VIRGO

Date Range: August 23–September 22

Element: earth

Ruling Planet: Mercury

Modality: mutable

Symbol: the virgin

Best Qualities: analytical, observant, organized, and practical

Challenging Qualities: critical, judgmental, perfectionist, and petty

Body Rulership: digestive system, intestines, pancreas, and spleen

Mantra: "I analyze."

Crystals: jade, peridot, serpentine, smoky quartz, sugilite, and unakite

Colors: earthy greens, floral pastels, and rich chocolates

Virgos are the second earth sign of the zodiac and are ruled by communicative Mercury. However, rather than being a master of verbal speech and articulating information, they are masters of the visual and information processing. For this reason, Virgos are known to be very observant, needing to know as much as possible before acting on anything. They love the arts—music, dance, writing, and film—because these allow Virgos an opportunity to dig deep into the symbolism and meaning behind what they see. Their attentive natures can sometimes make it seem as if they are being overly critical. This sign challenges us to think about what is going on and embrace an analytical mindset. As an earth sign, Virgo is a practical sign that is heavily committed to routine. Virgo placements will illustrate how you pay attention to deals and what you do with them.

LIBRA

Date Range: September 23–October 22

Element: air

Ruling Planet: Venus

Modality: cardinal

Symbol: the scales

Best Qualities: artistic, equal, expressive, and harmonious

Challenging Qualities: codependent, flaky, indecisive, and superficial

Body Rulership: kidneys and buttocks

Mantra: "I balance."

Crystals: lepidolite, morganite, opal, pink tourmaline, and rose quartz

Colors: pastels in all shades

Being the second air sign and second sign ruled by Venus, Libra aims to create balance and harmony in the world. The way they manifest this balance is with beauty. Connoisseurs of visual art, fashion, and overall aesthetics, Libras exude a charming creativity. They are coziest when draped in luxury, enjoying the finer things in life. Libra is the champion of equality, having a strong moral compass and desire for fairness and justice. However, in trying to remain balanced, Libras often find it difficult to make decisions, resulting in a flaky demeanor. Their greatest lesson is trusting their intuition when at a crossroads. Libra's energy challenges you to find balance in your life to reach inner harmony. Placements in Libra showcase where you find beauty in life and where you need to draw boundaries to achieve the harmony the sign craves.

SCORPIO

Date Range: October 23–November 21

Element: water

Ruling Planet: Mars (classical) and Pluto (modern)

Modality: fixed

Symbol: the scorpion

Best Qualities: charming, intense, mysterious, and passionate

Challenging Qualities: aggressive, jealous, manipulative, and secretive

Body Parts: genitals, the reproductive system, and hips

Mantra: "I desire."

Crystals: kunzite, labradorite, malachite, rhodochrosite, sodalite, and topaz

Colors: rich reds, hot pinks, deep purples, indigo, and black

Scorpios are symbolized by the scorpion, an elusive and venomous creature that thrives in the darkness and solitude. This sign rules over the areas of sex and death. Scorpios have magnetic personalities that draw others to them. They are fun, flirtatious, and make for loyal friends and advisers. At the same time, their intense nature can be tough to handle. They are deep thinkers, and as a water sign, they are deeply tapped into their emotions. At the same time, they are very independent, making them trust their intuition over evidential findings. In nature, the scorpion is an opportunistic predator, which sheds light on Scorpio's manipulative nature. Scorpio placements illustrate the part of your life that craves passion, thrills, and danger. The sign challenges you to question what it is you desire, how badly you want it, and to what lengths you will go to get it.

SAGITTARIUS

Date Range: November 23–December 21

Element: fire

Ruling Planet: Jupiter

Modality: mutable

Symbol: the archer

Best Qualities: adventuresome spirit, fair, intellectual, and optimistic

Challenging Qualities: careless, dogmatic, forgetful, and inconsistent

Body Rulership: thighs, liver, pituitary gland, and sciatic nerve

Mantra: "I see."

Crystals: amethyst, malachite, smoky quartz, sodalite, and turquoise

Colors: yellow, orange, rust, brown, and purple

Sagittarius is a mutable fire sign, making it an adaptable wildfire. Ruled by the archer, Sags love travel and freedom, as illustrated by the arrow in flight. This sign revels in transformation and enjoys philosophical creativity. As a fire sign, Sags are charming, warm, and expressive, eager to make connections. Their emotional intelligence merges with creative passion and social cognizance, making them well-rounded. However, on their quest for finding truth, they can sometimes struggle with others' ideas and opinions. In this way, Sags can be a bit dogmatic, crushing empathy with ego. Sags are independent, adventurous, and big risk-takers. They work best when they are allowed to teach or share their ideas and findings. This sign challenges you to "see" not only what is in front of you, but also that which you seek to obtain. Sag placements illustrate the areas in your life where you seek freedom to run wild.

CAPRICORN

Date Range: December 22–January 19

Element: earth

Ruling Planet: Saturn

Modality: cardinal

Symbol: the sea goat

Best Qualities: ambitious, determined, disciplined, and hardworking

Challenging Qualities: condescending, arrogant, rigid, and unsatisfied

Body Rulership: bones/skeletal system, teeth, knees, and joints

Mantra: "I use."

Crystals: black tourmaline, garnet, onyx, ruby, and smoky quartz

Colors: green, silver, gold, and gray (money colors)

The cardinal earth sign of Capricorn is a ruler of material matter. Capricorns are a highly ambitious and determined sign that finds comfort in success. Being an earth sign, Caps are practical and grounded, loving the structure of material items for the achievement and success that comes from obtaining them. This sign is known for being career driven. Caps are quite competitive when it comes to obtaining their goals. They long to leave a legacy behind. This sign urges you to ask, "How do I want to be remembered?" and make sustained efforts to achieve your goals. Caps are also known to have very high standards and can have the tendency to appear emotionless, cold, and condescending. Capricorn placements indicate the areas of life where you have a great sense of responsibility. Tap into Capricornian energy when looking to become more organized, goal oriented, or disciplined.

AQUARIUS

Date Range: January 20–February 18

Element: air

Ruling Planet: Saturn (classical) and Uranus (modern)

Modality: fixed

Symbol: the water-bearer

Best Qualities: friendly, humanitarian, imaginative, and social

Challenging Qualities: aloof, chaotic, detached, and extremist

Body Rulership: calves, ankles, and circulatory system

Mantra: "I know."

Crystals: garnet, jasper, moss agate, opal, ruby in zoisite, and sugilite

Colors: shades of blue, yellow, orange, mint green, and pale pink

Aquarius is the rebellious visionary of the zodiac. Despite being a fixed sign, Aquarius loves to "spread" information and is considered a humanitarian. Aquarians are revolutionary thinkers who wish to be a stabilizing force for others. They aim to change society for the better. Their stubbornness is associated with their scorn for authority. It manifests as a need for freedom and an unwillingness to conform. While they can be somewhat introverted, they do enjoy social situations. However, their need for freedom sometimes results in them being loners. Their detached and nontraditional natures make them the "alien" of the zodiac signs. They have a unique interest in technology and its role in sharing information with others. Aquarian placements showcase an area of life that is centered on community and spreading new ideas. It is also the area of life where you may feel a bit different and do not fit in. Work with Aquarian energy to establish a sense of freedom.

PISCES

Date Range: February 19–March 20

Element: water

Ruling Planet: Jupiter (classical) and Neptune (modern)

Modality: mutable

Symbol: the fish

Best Qualities: compassionate, gentle, imaginative, and mystical

Challenging Qualities: escapist, sensitive, spiteful, and victim mentality

Body Rulership: hands and feet

Mantra: "I believe."

Crystals: aquamarine, coral, fluorite, jade, and ocean jasper

Colors: silvers, blue, lavender, and turquoise

The last sign of the zodiac is Pisces. Those born under this sign are sensitive and imaginative with a high capacity for empathy. Like other water signs, Pisces are extremely aware of their emotions. They are compassionate and creative creatures who use their emotions as an inspiration in creative pursuits. Highly intuitive, the sign dips into the waters of the collective unconscious—focusing their energy on their internal awareness. This sign often struggles with reality, preferring to get lost in fantastical states of mind. For this reason, they are not the best at addressing problems. At the same time, they are mutable, represented by two fish swimming in opposite directions, which showcases their flexibility as an emotional sign. Pisces must remember to stay grounded. Piscean placements showcase where you are mystical and connected to more spiritual aspects of the world. Use Pisces energy when looking to enhance your imagination or intuition.

YOUR BIG THREE

The Sun, the Moon, and Ascendant/rising signs are considered the "big three" planetary signs that have predominance in contemporary astrology. The Sun sign reflects your overall identity in this lifetime. It spotlights the energy that is most active in your personality—what you like and how you recharge. The Moon is linked to your inner needs. It is the emotional current that flows through you. The Moon is also connected to your instincts and intuition and how you see the world. The Ascendant, or rising sign, is represented by the zodiac sign that is at the eastern horizon during the time of birth. Directly on the edge of the first house, the Ascendant is sitting on your self-identity and personality. An energetic mask that you wear for the world, it is a reflection of how others see you.

THE PLANETS

Classical astrology was made up of only seven planets: the Sun, the Moon, Mercury, Venus, Mars, Jupiter, and Saturn. This was because Saturn is the most distant planet that can be seen with the naked eye. The ancients were unaware of the outer planets. That's why the astrological signs of Scorpio, Aquarius, and Pisces have two ruling planets—one for classical astrology and one for modern astrology. The seven classical planets were divided into two sections, the Sun, Moon, Mercury, Venus, and Mars being the personal planets, with Jupiter and Saturn—the largest—the social planets. The outer planets were discovered nearly 3,500 years later and are used in Western astrology to illustrate the collective unconscious. Each planet is linked to various forms of energy and given governance over the zodiac.

THE SUN

Day: Sunday

Colors: yellows, oranges, and gold

Zodiac Sign: Leo

House Ruler: Fifth House/the House of Pleasure

Transit Between Signs: one month

Planetary Return: one year to move through all signs (your birthday)

Planetary Retrogrades: N/A

Keywords: confidence, ego, identity, joy, manifestation, and vitality

THE MOON

Day: Monday

Colors: whites, silvers, creams, black, and gray

Zodiac Sign: Cancer

House Ruler: Fourth House/the House of Roots

Transit Between Signs: two to three days

Planetary Return: 13 times a year to move through all signs

Planetary Retrogrades: N/A

Keywords: emotions, habits, instinct, intuition, and subconscious

MERCURY

Day: Wednesday

Colors: yellows, blues, and purples

Zodiac Signs: Gemini and Virgo

House Ruler: Third House/the House of Communication and Sixth House/the House of Routine

Transit Between Signs: two to three weeks

Planetary Return: one year to move through all signs and is close to your birthday, but not the actual day

Planetary Retrogrades: three to four times a year, lasting about three weeks at a time

Keywords: communication, intellect, intelligence, mental function, and reason

VENUS

Day: Friday

Colors: pinks, coppers, greens, and turquoise

Zodiac Signs: Taurus and Libra

House Ruler: Second House/the House of Resources and the Seventh House/the House of Partnerships

Transit Between Signs: four to five weeks

Planetary Return: one year to move through all signs, but usually not on your birthday

Planetary Retrogrades: every year to year and a half, lasting on average six weeks

Keywords: art, beauty, love, luxury, money, and relationships

MARS

Day: Tuesday

Colors: red, burgundy, orange, and black

Zodiac Signs: Aries and Scorpio (classical)

House Ruler: First House/the House of Self

Transit Between Signs: six to seven weeks

Planetary Return: a year and a half to two years to move through all the signs

Planetary Retrogrades: every two years, lasting on average 10 weeks

Keywords: action, aggression, passion, physical, and strength

JUPITER

Day: Thursday

Colors: blues, greens, and purple

Zodiac Signs: Sagittarius and Pisces (classical)

House Ruler: Ninth House/the House of Exploration

Transit Between Signs: one year

Planetary Return: 12 years to move through all signs

Planetary Retrogrades: Every year to year and a half, lasting on average four months

Keywords: abundance, expansion, growth, luck, and opportunity

SATURN

Day: Saturday

Colors: blacks, grays, and maroon

Zodiac Signs: Capricorn and Aquarius (classical)

House Ruler: 10th House/the House of Legacy

Transit Between Signs: two and a half years

Planetary Returns: 28 to 29 years to move through all the signs

Planetary Retrogrades: once a year, lasting on average four to five months

Keywords: endings, law, loss, restriction, and structure

URANUS

Day: Wednesday

Colors: indigo, greens, and white

Zodiac Sign: Aquarius

House Ruler: 11th House/the House of Community

Transit Between Signs: six to seven years

Planetary Returns: 84 years to move through all the signs

Planetary Retrogrades: once a year, lasting on average five months

Keywords: awakening, change, independence, rebellion, and revolution

NEPTUNE

Day: Friday

Colors: blues, sea green, and silver

Zodiac Sign: Pisces

House Ruler: 12th House/the House of Spirituality

Transit Between Signs: 14 years

Planetary Return: 168 years to move through all the signs

Planetary Retrogrades: once a year, lasting on average
five months

Keywords: belief, dreams, fantasy, inspiration, and spirituality

PLUTO

Day: Tuesday

Colors: black, brown, and deep purple

Zodiac Sign: Scorpio

House Ruler: Eighth House/the House of Sex and Death

Transit Between Signs: 12 to 30 years

Planetary Returns: around 250 years to move through all signs

Planetary Retrogrades: once a year, lasting on average
five months

Keywords: death, extremes, intimacy, rebirth, and
transformation

PLANETARY RETROGRADES

I am going to bet you have heard of Mercury retrograde, an astrological phenomenon known as a time of pure communication chaos. All planets experience retrogrades, but Mercury has asserted itself to be the most felt. As the astrological ruler of communication and thought, Mercury's retrograde tends to cause communication bumps. During retrogrades (sometimes stylized as Rx), the planets appear to be moving backward from Earth. However, the planets do not actually move backward. A retrograde is an optical illusion during which the energetic associations of the affected planet will reverse. This typically comes with a set of obstacles, leaving us feeling like we are swimming upstream.

While retrogrades may be commonly perceived to be negative occurrences, the planet in retrograde is essentially calling for you to pause. It is a time of prudence. A time to carefully dot all of your i's and cross all of your t's. Therefore, it is often recommended to avoid rushing into anything during retrogrades. Following is a snapshot of what energetic expression is at hand during each planetary retrograde.

SUN: N/A

MOON: N/A

MERCURY: communication issues, electronic mishaps, travel delays; ill-advised to sign contracts

VENUS: relationship and resource issues; romantic pursuits may halt or be rough; existing relationships and partnerships will be rocky; you may experience low self-esteem because of your image or body; money issues or unexpected expenses may materialize

MARS: anger issues; stagnant drive, passion, libido, and all sources of physical energy

JUPITER: growth issues and feeling a lack of opportunity

SATURN: career, karma, and long-term goals issues; responsibilities may confine and restrict you

URANUS: independence issues and feeling your freedom is at risk, along with a lack of social situations; even fights with friends are possible during this time

NEPTUNE: spiritual issues, hazy intuition, and blocked dreams

PLUTO: transformative issues

THE 12 HOUSES

Starting just below the Ascendant, the houses move counter-clockwise, making up 12 distinct areas of life. The first four houses represent aspects of internal connections, the second four are about external connections, and the third four about societal connections. The houses are similar to spreads in tarot—their placement is meaningful. Where your planets and their distinguished signs are placed in the houses hold additional information on personality traits. For example, for communicative Gemini, a Venus (love) in Gemini (communication) can mean that the individual's loving nature is

expressed through their communication style. Now place this in the 11th house (community), and you get a person who is very communicative in expressing their love, which is anchored in friendships, social settings, and even aspects of technology. This person is likely very expressive of their admiration of friends and may be the person who rallies everyone together and uses social media to share their feelings with others.

THE FIRST HOUSE: THE HOUSE OF SELF

The first house is where it all begins. Marked by your Ascendant, this house defines who you are. It is the embodiment of your identity, ego, physical appearance, and persona in the world. Think of this house as a first impression. Being that this is the start of the houses, its energy is synonymous with Aries energy, and it is ruled by Mars. First-house placements are very bold and have a strong influence on how the world sees you. When planets transit through the first house, they will dramatically impact the person on a very individual basis. As a result, any astrological events that occur in the first house can alter your sense of self and identity.

THE SECOND HOUSE: THE HOUSE OF RESOURCES

The second house governs material and physical matters. It is deeply related to the senses, as well as other possessions that feel good and provide security. This is often associated with income and finances—how you obtain them, lend, borrow, and/or struggle with them. It also places emphasis on how you perceive value. This house is connected to Taurus energy and the planet Venus. Any placements in the second house will be deeply connected to material means and a sense of self-worth related to resources. When planets transit this house, it can indicate a shift in self-esteem or financial resources.

THE THIRD HOUSE: THE HOUSE OF COMMUNICATION

The third house is associated with Gemini and the planet Mercury, making it a house of intellect and communication. Therefore, this house is also connected to the varied ways of communicating, whether they be spoken or written. This house is connected to imagination and plays a part in how technology is used to store or transmit intelligence and communication. When natal planets are located in this house, individuals may be likely to use communication as a focal point in one area of their life. As planets transit through the third house, you may find communication is easier or more difficult depending on the planet.

THE FOURTH HOUSE: THE HOUSE OF ROOTS

The fourth house is associated with Cancer and the Moon and sits at the bottom of the natal chart. This house is marked by the Imum Coeli—or space where the ecliptic crosses the meridan. It is opposite of the Midheaven. Therefore, it represents the foundation of self—ruling over your origins, ancestry, and feelings of comfort. It is deeply anchored to your upbringing and connectedness to your mother or mother figure. It is also connected to inner emotions that have either helped or hindered personal growth. Natal planetary placement in this house will suggest a strong connection to family, and as planets transit through, changes in mood or relationship dynamics with family members may fluctuate.

THE FIFTH HOUSE: THE HOUSE OF PLEASURE

The fifth house governs areas of pleasure, romance, and enthusiasm. It is connected to creativity and how you find joy. It is ruled by the zodiac sign of Leo and the Sun. It is saturated in warmth and attraction of all kinds. This house showcases how an individual will have fun, exploring themes of creative fulfillment through entertaintment. It is also connected to flirtation, dating, and casual sex. Natal planetary placements in this house will often dictate how you perceive or like to have fun. When other planets transit through the fifth house, you may find creativity ebbs and flows, in addition to the potential for attracting new people into your life.

THE SIXTH HOUSE: THE HOUSE OF ROUTINE

The sixth house is anchored in mercurial Virgo's practicality and analysis. As a result, this house rules over routine: how we form habits and keep schedules. It is also linked to health and wellness and the daily routines associated with both, such as exercise, nutrition, and cleansing. It is through these routines that we learn our usefulness, be it to others, our jobs, or society itself. Natal sixth house placements are strongly focused on self-care and mental well-being. When other planets travel through the sixth house, you should pay attention to the structure and usefulness of that area of your life.

THE SEVENTH HOUSE: THE HOUSE OF PARTNERSHIP

The seventh house sits directly across from the first (self), symbolizing when one becomes two. This house is associated with Libra and Venus, rooting itself in the theme of the partnerships established in life—romantic, platonic, and business. Just as the first house sits on the Ascendant, the seventh is seated upon the Descendant, rounding out the bottom half of the natal chart, an area linked to the intimate worlds of self, money, communication, home, creativity, and health. The Descendant represents the qualities that you long for and admire in others. Natal placements in this house will illustrate a deep interest and need for partnerships throughout life. As planets transit through the seventh house, the area of life they govern will be focused on various partnerships and your relationship to them.

THE EIGHTH HOUSE: THE HOUSE OF SEX & DEATH

The eighth house deals with the realms of sex, death, and transformative rebirth. Ruled by Scorpio, Mars, and Pluto, this house is dark, but it is from this darkness that we can see the light. It is a deeply introspective house that also deals with our intimacy and vulnerability. This house is also associated with finances, loans, and the management of other people's money. Where the fifth house is connected to playful, unattached sexuality, this house governs passionate sexuality that is rooted in the deep bond between you and another, moving beyond making love and into something deeply spiritual and instinctual. Eighth-house placements will likely have fixations on what is taboo in the world, with interests in the supernatural and occult. When planets move through this house, it will be time to shake things up. Allow change to manifest and intimacy to form. Makeovers and redecorating are also good at this time.

THE NINTH HOUSE: THE HOUSE OF EXPLORATION

Associated with the traveling arrow of Sagittarius and expansive Jupiter, the ninth house is one of exploration and study. Deeply saturated in philosophy and truth, this house is about a yearning to learn. Whereas the third house rules over newfound cognitive ability and communication, the ninth house wishes to move beyond this to a higher level of mental stimulation. Natal placements will have a wanderlust to know and experience more and may be very intellectually studious and connoisseurs of travel. When planets travel through this house, the area they govern over your life will be exposed to new ideas and experiences.

THE 10TH HOUSE: THE HOUSE OF LEGACY

The 10th house begins at the very top of the birth chart, opposite your Imum Coeli. This point is known as the Midheaven, or Medium Coeli, which ultimately shows the career that is best suited for you. The 10th house is full of ambition when it comes to your career, reputation, influence, and power. It marks your contribution to society and what you leave behind—how you will be remembered. Linked to Capricorn and Saturn, it is influenced by the power of long-term goals. Natal planets in this house showcase the area of your life where you want to make a good impression and work to achieve it. Transits in this house denote changing success or failure in career or lifestyle.

THE 11TH HOUSE: THE HOUSE OF COMMUNITY

Anchored in the energy of Aquarius, Saturn, and Uranus, the 11th house rules over aspects of community. This house governs friendships, gatherings, and memberships, showcasing how you are received by society and your motives for being a part of different organizations. This house also deals with bettering society and ways to serve to humanity. Natal placements in this house will be focused on social settings and connection with certain aspects of society. The planet in this house will also indicate the area of your life that is most communal. Transits in this house from the 10th (legacy) will indicate how your social life is impacted by your career.

THE 12TH HOUSE: THE HOUSE OF SECRETS

The 12th house is the last in the natal chart and is home to the unseen spiritual forces that take root just below the surface of our lives. Associated with Pisces, Jupiter, and Neptune, this is a house of imagination, art, secrets, dreams, and hidden desires. It is the house where our unconscious beliefs are rooted in instinct. It is where we come face to face with our own self-sabotage. It is closely associated with addictions and getting lost in fantasies to escape reality. This said, it is also deeply connected to intuition and spiritual heritage. Natal placements in this house will generally showcase a part of your life that feels restriction and hidden enemies. Transits in the 12th house illuminate aspects of karma or highlight a period of illusion or confusion.

THE ASPECTS & PATTERNS

Aspects are important because they show how forces within your natal chart are working with or against each other. This can have a dramatic impact on a planetary placement and change the meaning altogether. This is because instead of one energetic theme, it multiplies or subtracts these qualities depending on the angles formed in the aspects. Aspects are given a margin in which they have influence; this is called an "orb." It is made of the number of degrees that an aspect can deviate in distance from the exact degree of the aspect. So, if an aspect is considered 180° apart, and the planets are apart by 175°, the -5° would be considered the orb.

COMMON ASPECTS

There are a handful of different aspects, but the ones that follow are most common and are frequently shown on natal charts.

Conjunction happens when two planets or astrological bodies are 0° apart, with an orb of 1 to 10°. When this occurs, both planets energetically link up and their energies blend. Depending on the placement, this combined energy may be harmonic or chaotic. For instance, a Sun and Venus conjunction can represent a personality that is fixated on love, beauty, and luxury, but the Sun dominates individuality, making love potential and partnerships scarce.

Sextile occurs when planets are 60° apart with an orb of 3 to 4°. This aspect shows harmony between the planetary energies.

Square is when planets are at a 90° angle to each other, with an orb of 5 to 10°. This aspect causes a sharp tension between their energies and the areas of life they affect.

Trine happens when three planets form a 120° triangle, with an orb of 5 to 10°. Similar to a sextile, this aspect is very harmonious, as the three planets work together and highlight areas of innate talent.

Opposition is when two planets are 180° apart with an orb of 5 to 10°. This puts the energies between the two planets at odds, making for an internal struggle. But opposites attract, right? The key with any opposition is to establish balance between the energy of both planets.

ASPECT PATTERNS

The different aspects in your chart differentiate themselves in various patterns that offer even more cosmic insight into your astrological portrait. When interpreting your chart, look for the following patterns.

T Square is formed when two planets are in opposition at 180° and is squared by a third at 90°. This creates a T shape in the chart. The third planet between the opposition is considered the focal planet, which places additional tension on the opposition. The focal planet becomes a release for the tension and ultimately pushes the person into action.

Grand Cross is a T square with an additional planet 90° between an opposition on the other side. Essentially, four planets are all 90° apart, forming a perfect cross in the center of a natal chart. Having two intersecting oppositions produces even more tension on your chart. Note that there are three possible formations for a Grand Cross, because each planet will be one sign of the same modality (example: a cardinal grand cross will include planets in Aries, Cancer, Libra, and Capricorn). The best solution is to find balance by doing what another modality does best. Cardinal Grand Crosses should be more flexible; Fixed Grand Crosses need to move and adapt; and Mutable Grand Crosses need to anchor their energy by grounding firmly.

Grand Trine creates a perfect triangle of three planets all in the same element. This pattern in a chart brings a specific flavor of luck and opportunity to an individual. This is a relatively rare pattern that has been called the Triangle of Talent. Fire signs with this pattern are enthusiastic artists full of pride. Earth signs with Grand Trines are deep and sensual artists fixated on the physical world. Air signs with Grand Trines are intellectual artists who are deeply connected to mental stimuli. Water signs with this pattern are reflective artists fixated on intimate dreamworlds.

Kite is essentially Grand Trine with an additional point that is in opposition to one of the triangle's points. This extra point creates additional tension in your chart and can ultimately become a motivating force that creates a drive to excel in your trine's talent.

Yod looks like a skinnier trine. These patterns are very rare and offer insight into a cosmic destiny that you are driven toward in life. It is sometimes called the Finger of God and spiritually connects to the purpose you are being pointed to in life.

Mystic Rectangle refers to an opposition of two aspects that are combined with two trine and two sextile aspects. This pattern showcases much success in a person's lifetime. There is harmony created between trine and sextile aspects, with just enough stress placed on the opposition points to create motivation for chasing dreams.

INTERPRETING YOUR NATAL CHART

Up until now, you have heard a lot about natal, or birth, charts. Well, the time has come to find and interpret your own! The best way to look at your natal chart is like a cosmic fingerprint—it is uniquely yours, exemplifying your personality traits and cosmic influence over your life. Follow the instructions below to start understanding the energies that cosmically make you the mystical, magical witch you are!

ACCESSING YOUR NATAL CHART

Many astrologers stress the importance of finding your accurate birth time as this will determine all of the house placements as well as the degrees of the ascendant, Imum Coeli, descendant, and Medium Coeli. Because of this, medical records that contain your exact time of birth are preferred, as the difference of a minute can drastically change your natal chart. However, this is not always feasible. If you do not have access to this due to missing records, adoption, etc. do not fret! Use what information you do know to build your chart. Various websites and apps let you access your natal chart for free. My go-to site is Astro.com, which allows you to enter several variables as you calculate, and show the different transits for the day in question. Alternatively, Astro-Charts.com is a good one that gives a bit more detail about your placements.

You will be asked various questions about your date, time, and place of birth to calculate the positions of your chart. If you are unsure of the time, don't fret—that only really applies to your Ascendant or rising sign. There is a chance it could also affect your Moon sign. But even without a time of birth, you can still gain a better understanding of yourself through the other placements.

EXAMINE YOUR PLACEMENTS

After generating your natal chart, you can begin to examine your placements. Look and make note of where each of your planets and other astronomical bodies are. To start, pick a planet, look up what it represents, what sign it is in, and the house. For example, if your Moon is in Libra in the first house, read the characteristics for the Moon sign, Libra, and the first house to get a bigger picture for interpretation. In this scenario, your identity (house) would be very much lined up with your emotions (planet: Moon), which will be heavily saturated in themes of partnership, beauty, aesthetics, and harmony (sign: Libra). Also, make note of the element and modality of the sign for additional context on how the placement operates. From here, draw calculations on the accuracy of your finding and move to the next planet or celestial body.

LOOK FOR ASPECTS & PATTERNS

Look at how the planets are positioned in your chart. Examine the aspects. Are there any conjunctions or oppositions? Do you have any patterns like a Grand Trine or Yod? Take these aspects and their patterns into consideration as you review.

RECORD YOUR FINDINGS

Write down all your signs, planets, houses, aspects, and patterns. Putting pen to paper will help you better understand your placements for further reflection. Make notes on what makes sense and those findings that have left you puzzled. If you have conflict in your chart, make note of that and look at ways in which you can minimize tension to create balance.

EXAMINE TRANSITS

Once you have interpreted your natal chart, you can begin mapping the daily transits, the movement the planets make through the houses. Observing these in connection to where your natal planets are positioned will help you forecast your future. To do this, use astrological sites like those previously mentioned to see the planetary positions for the day or a day in the future. The transits will appear on the outside of your natal chart, while your natal planets remain inside the circle. Take into consideration the sign and house of the transiting planets and how they interact with your natal placements. Is a planet experiencing a return? Is there a square or opposition taking place? This can give you an idea of what kind of energy is in store for you. For example, if Saturn's transit creates an opposition to your natal Venus, restrictions and frustrations in partnership may be in store for you. Likewise, if the transiting Sun is conjunct to your natal Venus, your love life and ability to create beauty in the natural world may come into focus. If Mars is square in your Midheaven, you may find an increased desire to take action toward your career. Transits can be confusing at first, but as with any aspect of astrology, practice makes perfect. Later on, in part 2, you will learn about the general energy of each transit and simple suggestions for magical practice.

KEY TAKEAWAYS

Having digested all the information in this chapter about the different parts and pieces that make up the puzzle of your natal chart, I'm sure your head is spinning. That is perfectly understandable and okay! Go back and read over the sections again or enhance your reading with additional research. Nevertheless, here are several key takeaways as we move to the next chapter on spellcraft considerations.

- **It's not just about your Sun sign.** There are many other planets, asteroids, and their positions that make an impact on your personality, compatibility, and more!

- **Astrological patterns offer further insight into your cosmic makeup.** There are various patterns that can affect how the signs and planets interact. Depending on the distance between planets, their energetic qualities may be enhanced or canceled in your chart. This is one reason why certain qualities might not automatically feel like a fit. This is also influential in understanding compatibility.

- **There are multiple ways to obtain your natal chart.** Online astrology software takes the hard work out of creating your natal chart. See the resources section of this book for some suggestions.

- **Transits play an instrumental role.** This is how you can create horoscopes and help map out your desires magically. As the planets move, they create additional potentials for influence. Tracking these will help you time your magical efforts.

CHAPTER 4

CONSIDERATIONS FOR SPELLCASTING

While this book is more eclectic in its approach and does not adhere to one style of witchcraft, there are standard tools, materials, and ingredients that can be called upon for astrology and witchcraft. This chapter will explore the various ways a witch can time or craft spells by using aspects of the natural world.

THE WHEEL OF THE YEAR

The Wheel of the Year is a symbolic reference of important holidays observed by pagans, Wiccans, and witches. The wheel follows Celtic influences in accordance with the seasonal shifts experienced in the Northern Hemisphere. These days follow the cyclical theme of nature's life, death, and rebirth and are called Sabbats—four being considered seasonal festivals and four solar festivals.

The seasonal festivals take place on the equinoxes and solstices when the Sun enters a new cardinal sign at 0°. The solar festivals, on the other hand, are also linked to when the Sun enters a fixed sign at 0°. Each year, the exact dates of each occurrence change slightly; however, the solar festivals (Samhain, Imbolc, Beltane, and Lammas) have all been assigned general days for mass celebration. When it comes to working magic with astrology, the degrees and signs matter. Following is a quick snapshot of the Wheel of the Year, its celebrated dates, astrological timing, themes, and celebration ideas.

SABBATS

SAMHAIN (HALLOWEEN)

Celebrated Date: October 31

True Astrological Date: Sun at 15° Scorpio

Themes: The Witch's New Year, a time of death and rebirth, the decline or death of sunlight and when the veils between worlds open.

Celebration Ideas: Honor your ancestors with spirit work. Use divination as a tool to reflect on yourself and find new opportunities for rebirth.

YULE (WINTER SOLSTICE)

Celebrated Date: December 20–23

True Astrological Date: Sun at 0° Capricorn

Themes: The longest night of the year, a time of silence and introspection, marked by celebrations with friends and family.

Celebration Ideas: Burn a Yule log. Reflect on your legacy. Have a witchy slumber. Party with those near and dear to you. Bake cookies. Celebrate your time together.

IMBOLC (CANDLEMAS)

Celebrated Date: February 2

True Astrological Date: Sun at 15° Aquarius

Themes: A time of new beginnings and inspiration and to rejuvenate your soul and plan for the coming year.

Celebration Ideas: Declutter or redecorate for the upcoming season. Meditate by candlelight to usher in the new light of the Sun's return. Reconnect with your community as winter wanes.

OSTARA (VERNAL EQUINOX)

Celebrated Date: March 20–23

True Astrological Date: Sun at 0° Aries

Themes: The rebirth of fertile nature and a time for planting seeds for growth and opportunity.

Celebration Ideas: Celebrate ambition and drive for change. Make wish lists of goals and opportunities to come. Spend time in nature.

BELTANE (MAY DAY)

Celebrated Date: May 1

True Astrological Date: Sun at 15° Taurus

Themes: A time for creation and creativity, this day represents the union and marriage of the Sun and Earth, bringing love, sexuality, and pleasure into focus.

Celebration Ideas: A traditional time to light bonfires and dance around the maypole, engage in joyous activities that give you pleasure. Love and sex magic rituals are common. Create a new sensual incense or oil blend.

LITHA (SUMMER SOLSTICE)

Celebrated Date: June 20–23

True Astrological Date: Sun at 0° Cancer

Themes: The longest day of the year, a time to energize the self with the warmth and vitality of the season and spend time with friends, family, and those who give comfort.

Celebration Ideas: Spend time cooling off in the water, perform dream magic, and leave offerings to the spirits of the place where you practice. Focus on your home and the comfort and joy it brings.

LAMMAS (LUGHNASADH)

Celebrated Date: August 1

True Astrological Date: Sun at 15° Leo

Themes: The first harvest, a time to celebrate the crops you have grown.

Celebration Ideas: Celebrate your achievements. Reflect on your doings and how you have been seen.

MABON (AUTUMNAL EQUINOX)

Celebrated Date: September 20–23

True Astrological Date: Sun at 0° Libra

Themes: The final harvest.

Celebration Ideas: Celebrate your abundance. Perform rituals of gratitude for the blessings and challenges you have overcome.

While the Wheel of the Year's European origins made for the perfect symbolic celebrations, not all locations experience the same seasonal changes in the typical way the wheel is mapped out. For example, Texas and Florida do not experience the same extremes in seasonal weather that Chicago and New York do. Major cities in the United States might not even physically see the agricultural effects outlined by the wheel. For this reason, many witches are now crafting their own Wheel of the Year based on their physical locations. One of the best ways to create your alternative wheel is to examine different seasonal changes, events, or festivals that occur in your area around the astrological timing of the wheel.

THE PHASES OF THE MOON

The Moon is a beloved force that witches use to map their intentions and energy patterns. So beloved is it that I have written two books on the subject: *Moon Spells for Beginners* and *The Complete Book of Moon Spells*. Being the closest astrological body to Earth and having a direct impact on gravity, mating and hunting rituals, and various other effects, it is no wonder that the Moon is considered a source of celestial magic beyond its astrological meaning.

In addition to the eight Sabbats, many witches also conduct monthly lunar rituals called Esbats. These are traditionally performed at the new and/or full moon phases. However, each phase can be seen as a symbolic time to conjure magic.

- **New Moon:** A time to set intentions

- **Waxing Crescent:** A time to focus on taking action

- **First Quarter:** A time to make decisions to bring your magic to fruition

- **Waxing Gibbous:** A time to get specific about your magical intentions

- **Full Moon:** A time to glow and celebrate the abundance of lunar energy

- **Waning Gibbous:** A time to express gratitude

- **Last Quarter:** A time to let go and forgive

- **Waning Crescent:** A time to release what no longer serves you

PLANETARY TIMING

When casting spells, consider specific days of the week to maximize your magical efforts. Each of the seven classical planets rules over one day of the week and two periods of the day. For example, it is traditional to do love spells on Friday (the day ruled by Venus, the planet of love) or during the planetary hour of Venus.

The planetary hours can be a bit tricky to nail down at first, but essentially, the planetary ruler of the day is the planet that starts at sunrise. Each day is associated with the seven major planets from ancient time. Each of these planets is given rulership for a section of time in the day. This is considered a planetary hour. These hours will be different depending on your location. You can use apps or online programs to determine the hours. However, the general rule is that whichever planet rules the day is the planet that starts at sunrise for that day. An hour later, it moves into another planet. Therefore, there are two times of day when a planetary hour exists. The order of the planetary hours is Sun, Venus, Mercury, Moon, Saturn, Jupiter, Mars, and back to the Sun.

So, if you wanted to work a special type of magic, but were unable to on a specific day, a good modifier would be to do it on a day when you can tap into the planetary hour best suited for your magical working. You can also combine hours and days to maximize your efforts. For example, going back to love spells, let's say you wanted to call forth a passionate and sexy new lover—something that combined love (Venus) and lust (Mars). You could do a spell on a Tuesday in the hour of Venus or on a Friday in the hour of Mars. To help calculate these, I recommend using the Planetary Hours Calculator on Astrology.com.

TOOLS TO LEVEL UP YOUR PRACTICE

It has been said many times that the only tools you need to practice witchcraft are yourself and your will. However, a variety of tools are commonly used by witches to enhance their spellcraft and rituals. Beginner witches often find that tools help anchor the mind and their intentions. However, as you become more adept in your practice, you may not feel drawn to using a bunch of tools, and that's totally acceptable. Regardless of which tools you use, it is best to reserve them only for your magical practice.

CANDLES

When we imagine casting a spell, candles are usually a go-to for Hollywood imagery, and with good reason! Candles are used to represent the element of fire. Different-colored candles can be used in spells based on your desired manifestation:

Pink: compassion, friendship, and love

Red: passion, power, and strength

Orange: ambition, confidence, and courage

Yellow: intelligence, happiness, and logic

Green: fertility, health, and prosperity

Blue: communication, emotional healing, and harmony

Purple: psychic power, spirituality, and wisdom

Brown: comfort, home, and stability

Black: banishment, binding, and protection

White: peace, purity, and reflection

Gold: abundance, personal power, and success

Silver: glamour, intuition, and psychic ability

Candles come in a variety of shapes and sizes that might influence your spellcraft. While there are many ways to practice candle magic, one of the most common ways to use candles in magic is by dressing them. This can be achieved by carving special sigils, symbols, or astrological glyphs into the wax with a knife or pin, anointing them with special oils, and even brushing them with powdered herbs. Sprinkle a bit of mica on your candles to add an additional layer of attraction. Once adorned, the candle is then lit as part of the spell. Always be sure to practice fire safety when using candles. For instance, never place a candle or open flame near other objects that could catch fire, and never leave a burning candle unattended in a room.

INCENSE

Incense is used as a representation of air. The smoke and smell of incense trigger both physical and metaphysical energies that can aid in magical work. Incense can be burned as sticks, cones, or even made yourself by grinding herbs, gums, and resins into fine powders that can then be sprinkled on top of lit charcoal discs. If doing the latter, you may also wish to place a bit of aluminum foil between the burning disc and herbal blend to minimize burn time and reduce the amount of smoke that is produced.

CRYSTALS

Crystals are used in spellcraft for their energetic qualities. Not only does each crystal help connect to the element of earth, but they also possess unique energies that align with different qualities, like love, prosperity, protection, and focus. They can also be applied to astrology and connected to the planets and signs. They can be added to spell bags, buried in the earth, arranged in grid formations for charging and summoning, held during rituals to amplify energy and focus, or even worn to harmonize your manifestations.

HERBS

Various plants, flowers, seeds, nuts, fruit, spices, gums, and resins are used in spells and rituals for their energetic correspondences. They are the most common ingredient used in spellcraft and can be eaten or drank in teas, applied topically for healing, added to magical oil blends, dried and crushed into incense blends, and grown around your home.

ESSENTIAL OILS

Essential oils are made by extracting and concentrating the chemical components of herbs. They are often used in perfumes or other oil blends to anoint yourself or other magical objects to energize them. They can also be used in aromatherapy to stimulate relaxation and sensuality through smell.

ATHAME & WAND

Witches have two tools to direct energy in spells and rituals. An athame is a magnetized ritual blade. Traditionally, it has a black handle and is double-sided. Historically, it is not used to cut physical matter, but is reserved for focusing energy. However, many modern witches use their athames to cut or carve ingredients. A wand is usually constructed from a branch or metal and fastened with crystals, feathers, symbols, or other magical enhancements. For many, the athame and wand are used interchangeably, and it is not uncommon for a practicing witch to prefer one over the other, or neither for that matter. You can also use the index finger of your dominant hand to accomplish the same things.

ALTAR TILE

An altar tile acts as a blessing plate in spells or rituals. Traditionally it is a circular object constructed from wood, clay, or metal with the pentacle—or witch's star—in the center. However, there are many magical symbols that might resonate with you more, like the triquetra, Egyptian ankh, or even the sigil associated with a deity. You can even make one yourself! Have fun and be creative.

MORTAR & PESTLE

A mortar and pestle is an instrument used to help grind herbs into fine powders. These powders can then be used as incense on lit charcoal discs, added to magical bags, sprinkled on candles, or added to magical baths. They are readily available at most cooking supply and home-good stores.

CAULDRON

Another stereotypical witch tool, the cauldron is a vessel used to hold important items during rituals, like large candles, flowers, or other offerings. Additionally, it can be used to hold fire and burn petitions during spells. A great alternative is to use a fireproof cooking pot.

CHALICE

A chalice is a drinking vessel used for liquid offerings and libations in spells or rituals. It can be made of silver, metal, glass, crystal, or wood.

BOOK OF SHADOWS

A Book of Shadows contains magical rituals, spells, and information unique to a witch's personal practice. However, your magical record-keeping can be done in a simple journal or even a three-ring binder, which would provide flexibility in changing out items or including folders with pockets to hold magical ingredients. Some witches opt for an electronic Book of Shadows that is saved privately. How you record your magical and astrological progress is entirely up to you.

ALTARS & SHRINES

Altars act as the workstation for a witch's craft. They house all your tools and ingredients for spellcraft or ceremonial ritual. They can be permanent or erected only when needed. Many witches with permanent altars rearrange and decorate them in accordance with the seasons. Shrines, on the other hand, are devoted places of worship for deities or spirits. Certain traditions have rules about the cardinal direction an altar should be facing and where the items on it should be located. Solitary practice allows you to follow your intuition and construct your altar in whatever manner you see fit.

ASTROLOGY WITH CRYSTALS, ESSENTIAL OILS & HERBS

The following crystals, essential oils, and herbs can enhance the positive aspects of each zodiac archetype.

ARIES

Crystals: aquamarine, bloodstone, carnelian, diamond, garnet, and pyrite

Essential Oils: cedar, clove, dragon's blood, frankincense, musk, and pine

Herbs: carnation, cinnamon, geranium, red pepper, tulip, and wormwood

TAURUS

Crystals: amber, aventurine, emerald, lapis, rhodonite, and rose quartz

Essential Oils: cardamom, patchouli, pomegranate, rose, strawberry, and vanilla

Herbs: apple, avocado, grape, lilac, mint, and olive

GEMINI

Crystals: agate, apophyllite, celestite, citrine, opal, and tiger's eye

Essential Oils: almond, clover, daffodil, lavender, lily, and mulberry

Herbs: anise, dill, lemongrass, marjoram, parsley, and skullcap

CANCER

Crystals: chrysoprase, moonstone, ocean jasper, opal, pearl, and selenite

Essential Oils: bay, eucalyptus, lotus, myrrh, sandalwood, and watermelon

Herbs: aloe, coconut, cucumber, gardenia, jasmine, and lemon

LEO

Crystals: amber, citrine, peridot, ruby, sunstone, and tiger's eye

Essential Oils: copal, frankincense, marigold, pepper, and sandalwood

Herbs: juniper, grapefruit, orange, pineapple, rue, and sunflower

VIRGO

Crystals: jade, peridot, serpentine, smoky quartz, sugilite, and unakite

Essential Oils: almond, bergamot, lavender, mint, peppermint, and pomegranate

Herbs: blackberry, caraway, dill, lemongrass, lily of the valley, and verbena

LIBRA

Crystals: lepidolite, morganite, opal, pink tourmaline, rose quartz, and topaz

Essential Oils: bergamot, cherry, geranium, lime, rose, and sweet pea

Herbs: catnip, lilac, mugwort, pansy, rooibos, and thyme

SCORPIO

Crystals: labradorite, malachite, rhodochrosite, sodalite, topaz, and unzite

Essential Oils: basil, ginger, musk, pine, sage, and tobacco

Herbs: allspice, coriander, hibiscus, mustard, thistle, and wormwood

SAGITTARIUS

Crystals: amethyst, malachite, smoky quartz, shungite, sodalite, and turquoise

Essential Oils: basil, clove, frankincense, neroli, star anise, and tea tree

Herbs: dandelion, echinacea, nutmeg, peach, saffron, and willow

CAPRICORN

Crystals: black tourmaline, garnet, malachite, onyx, ruby, and smoky quartz

Essential Oils: bergamot, cypress, frankincense, juniper, myrrh, and sandalwood

Herbs: caraway, chamomile, comfrey, rosemary, tarragon, and vervain

AQUARIUS

Crystals: garnet, jasper, moss agate, opal, ruby in zoisite, and sugilite

Essential Oils: benzoin, black pepper, cedar, peppermint, rose, and violet

Herbs: comfrey, orchid, rosemary, star anise, thyme, and valerian

PISCES

Crystals: amethyst, aquamarine, coral, fluorite, jade, and ocean jasper

Essential Oils: jasmine, juniper, lemon, sandalwood, sweet pea, and wisteria

Herbs: chamomile, passionflower, nutmeg, seaweed, skullcap, and valerian

STOCKING YOUR MAGICAL CUPBOARD

In addition to the specific tools witches use, there are some ingredients you should stock up on and have readily available for your witchcrafting. Curating a magical cabinet is much like stocking your kitchen with essential ingredients. Before engaging in any of the spells or rituals in part 2, look them over and create a shopping list that corresponds to the general or specialty ingredients needed, most of which can be broken down into the following list. Pay attention to your intuition; if something catches your eye, add it to your list as a must-have item. If this list appears intimidating, keep in mind that you should only get what you believe will be most useful to your craft.

- Almanac to track planetary movements
- Bell or gong to clear and summon energy
- Bottles and bowls to hold magical ingredients
- Candleholders in different sizes and shapes to hold your candles
- Candles in different sizes, shapes, and colors to use in magic
- Charcoal discs to burn blended incenses
- Cords in various colors to use for knot magic
- Crystals such as amethyst, citrine, clear quartz, smoky quartz, and rose quartz to amplify energy

- Electronic device to stream music for meditation

- Epsom salt for magical baths and beauty rituals

- Essential oils to blend for magical purposes

- Feathers to represent the element of air and fan incense smoke

- Heatproof bowl (as an alternative for a cauldron) to safely burn items in spellcasting

- Herbs (fresh and dried) to use in spells

- Incense (stick, cone, or blended) that is commonly used in spellcasting, such as dragon's blood, frankincense, lavender, nag champa, rose, and sandalwood

- Jojoba or fractionated coconut oil to use as a carrier oil for diluting harsh essential oils and stretching their fragrance

- Lighter or matches to light candles and burn items of importance in spells

- Measuring cups/spoons to portion ingredients

- Paper and pens/markers in various colors to write magical petitions

- Sachets or cloth bags for making herbal blends and magical bath teas

- Sea salt to add to spellwork and use in magical cleansings to dissolve negativity

- Smudge stick or palo santo to clear and cleanse energy

CREATING A NATAL ALTAR

It is not uncommon for witches to have various altars or shrines in their homes. Creating a natal altar that is built around your birth chart can further connect you with planetary energies in a personal way. You could use your natal chart as an altar tile and then position various candles, crystals, incense, etc., around it to match your chart. For example, a fire-sign placement can be marked by a candle in the color that is associated with that sign. An earth-sign placement can be represented by a crystal corresponding to your placement's sign. Incense in the scent associated with air signs can be burned in its position, and a water bowl can be placed in the position of a water sign. If any spellwork you are doing around the planets has leftover pieces, such as a candle that needs to be relit for additional days or a magical bag, they can also be added to the space to further align with your own planetary energy. Have fun and be creative while anchoring your magical goals in a visual representation of your chart.

FORMS OF DIVINATION

Divination is a practice that many witches use to gain clarity and insight about themselves or situations. Just as horoscopes are used to foresee the future and plan accordingly, there are a variety of other techniques you can incorporate into your astrological witchcraft to cultivate your intuition and psychic abilities. It is also a good idea to use divination to gauge the unseen forces at hand and help decide if there will be a favorable outcome to a magical working.

TAROT & ORACLE CARDS

The tarot is a medieval esoteric practice in which 78 cards are used for self-discovery, reflection, and to answer questions about the future. The cards are shuffled, and a select number are drawn into a spread. The placements provide overall meaning to the reading in the same way that houses do for planets in astrology. The definition of one card and its placement may change based on the surrounding cards. The Rider-Waite deck is commonly used, and all other decks use the Rider-Waite deck as a prototype. Oracle cards are a more laid-back version of tarot cards. Oracle decks contain cards with more distinct meanings. To achieve more clarity, some witches combine an oracle card reading with a tarot card reading.

SCRYING

Scrying is a divinatory technique used to "see" things on a reflective surface. Traditionally this is done with a black mirror or piece of polished obsidian. However, it can also be done with crystal balls, a bowl of water, regular mirrors, candle flames, and even the night sky. You may not actually "see" something play out like a scene in a movie or on television. Instead, this technique will cause ideas, feelings, or images to organically populate your mind.

PENDULUMS

Pendulums are weighted items attached to a chain and suspended in air by the user so that the item at the end of the chain can swing freely, guiding you in the right direction. Ask yes or no questions about which you wish to receive guidance. Remaining in a fixed position, close your eyes and focus on your query. Take note of the movements the pendulum makes. Back-and-forth movements or clockwise circular motions are considered a yes response, whereas side-to-side or counterclockwise movements are considered no replies. Pendulums can be purchased online or created at home using something as simple as a pendant on a chain.

PREPARING FOR YOUR SPELLCRAFT

Besides having the right ingredients and tools, there are other aspects of preparation needed for spellcasting. First, always check your mental and physical health before doing any spellwork to ensure that you are clearly focused and not distracted in any way. If you are coming home after a stressful day of work, jacked up on adrenaline or frustration, it might not be the best time to perform a spell, as the hostile mood from the day could impact your results. Likewise, if you are not feeling well and have low energy, consider doing your spell when you feel better and more able to manifest.

Be mindful of the location where you choose to perform the spell. Work in a relaxed and unobtrusive setting to keep your attention focused on the spell's goal. As appealing as it may seem to perform an evocative ceremony in the woods or on the beach, you should always find a safe site where you will not be exposed to harm from others, the elements, or animals. Likewise, be sure to have the proper privacy at home, away from roommates, children, pets, or other family members who might distract you.

Deciding what you plan to wear for your spell can be another fun and meaningful element. You may wish to dress in a color that corresponds to the magic you are conjuring to add an additional layer of energy. Many witches save their magic for special costumes or perform it naked, or sky clad—being clad only by the sky. If you choose a magical ensemble, be sure that it offers comfort and practicality. Dressing up in fringe and flowing capes may look and feel fantastic, but you don't want to burn yourself or your home down while wandering around a circle of lit candles.

Creating a magical playlist can significantly improve your spellcasting mood. If you decide to listen to music, choose music that doesn't distract from your work and instead enhances the intensity being expressed, either in instrumentation or lyrically. This is particularly effective with planetary magic, as NASA has been able to capture unique sounds from each planet through radio emissions and sound waves. These hauntingly beautiful noises make for great background music in meditations and spellcraft and are readily available online. Additionally, it might be helpful to prerecord guided meditations that you can play while you practice so you don't have to read a meditation script while practicing your craft.

Bathing or showering before any magical activity is a good way to physically cleanse yourself in preparation for your spell. However, this may not always be feasible. An alternative would be to cleanse your body with a smudging wand, piece of palo santo, magical spray, or incense smoke to center and align your energy. It is also a good idea to do this in the general area in which you perform the spell to clear the energy for your work.

KEY TAKEAWAYS

Understanding the ingredients of witchcraft is key to a successful practice. Having now explored the components needed to prepare for your spells, here are some key takeaways before you start witch-crafting your astrological magic in part 2.

- **The natural world provides an abundance of power.** The ebb and flow of the seasons, phases of the Moon, plants, and crystals can all be used in witchcraft as energy sources.

- **There are many tools of witchcraft, but the most important is you.** Your spells and rituals are infused by the intent with which you fuel them. That said, the various tools and ingredients can direct and enhance energy.

- **It is not *only* intuition.** Understanding magical correspondences will allow you to improvise with the right tools or other ingredients. Avoid making substitutions without first determining the energetic effects of the item you are using as a substitution.

- **Prepare ahead of time.** Be mindful of what you're doing before you start. Be conscientious of what magical ingredients you plan to use, the timing, location, clothing, and all other aspects that you can control.

PART II

SPELLS, PRACTICES & RITUALS

Welcome to part 2 of *Astrology for Witches*. As I'm sure you have discovered by now, astrology is a useful tool for witches looking to level up their practice, harness even more of the energy of the universe, and expand their magical practice. So are you ready to get your witch on with some planetary magic? Part 2 features 10 chapters, one for each of the planets.

CHAPTER 5

THE SUN: CONFIDENCE & PERSONAL POWER

The Sun is the conductor of your birth chart's symphony. As the core of our solar system, it astrologically energizes your identity. Physically, the Sun's beaming light provides vitamin D, which helps heal and refresh our bodies and moods. It is the most powerful planet in astrology, determining how you express yourself, find joy in life, and rejuvenate yourself. This chapter explores several magical techniques you can perform using the Sun's energy for confidence, personal power, and success. At the end of this chapter, you will find an overview of magical and mundane themes to consider with the Sun's transits so that you can make the most of your astrological spellcraft!

SOLAR MEDITATION

The following meditation is designed to help you tap into the Sun's astrological energy and establish your identity. Perform it when you feel you have lost yourself or need extra fuel for your willpower. Perform this meditation during the day, when you can sit in the Sun's warmth.

MATERIALS

Orange tea

Laptop or smartphone
  (optional)

Cushion or yoga mat to sit on

Lighter/match

Orange incense and lighter/
  matches

Orange oil

Journal and pen

INSTRUCTIONS

1. Brew a cup of orange tea. Pour it into a cup and find a comfortable and silent place where you can be touched by the Sun's rays.

2. Play ASMR (autonomous sensory meridian response) or white noise audio of Sun sounds found in my public Planetary Magic Meditation Playlist on YouTube (see Resources on page 174).

3. Sit in a relaxed stance. Light the incense and fan the smoke in your direction. Apply a small amount of oil to your wrists and clavicle.

4. Take a sip of your tea. Close your eyes and breathe deeply through your nose for 10 seconds before slowly exhaling through your mouth.

continued

5. Visualize the Sun glowing powerfully and radiantly. Focus on the vital role the Sun plays for the world and reflect on the ways in which it astrologically energizes your life. Consider the following: Who am I? What defines me? How do I show up in the world? How am I seen? How can I represent my best self better?

6. Feel the Sun's power set you aflame during your meditation, invigorating your answers.

7. Remain seated in meditation for a minimum of 30 minutes before slowly coming back to consciousness. Record any revelations in your journal.

SUNRISE CONFIDENCE SPELL

This is a simple spell to perform any morning you are in need of a confidence boost.

MATERIALS

Citrine, sunstone, or tiger's eye
  crystal

INSTRUCTIONS

1. Take your crystal to a window or outside just before sunrise so that you may greet the Sun.

2. Hold the crystal in both palms, gripping it tightly to your solar plexus, the space between your heart and belly button. Visualize your day unfolding with you moving forward in supreme confidence. While doing this say: "Oh, mighty sun, I call on thee. Flames of power, engulf me. Ignite my confidence for all to see. Now is the time, and empowerment is mine. I am ready to shine!"

3. Face the sunrise to the east and perform a pentagram salute by tracing the five-pointed star over your head and torso. Touch your third eye with the index finger of your dominant hand and trace a line from your forehead to your right breast. Now trace another line across your chest to your left shoulder, then the right shoulder, down to your left breast, and back to your forehead.

4. Take three deep breaths, in through your nose and out through your mouth.

5. Carry the crystal with you throughout the day as an anchor for your goal and a reminder that all of the Sun's power is beaming through you.

CANDLE SPELL FOR PERSONAL POWER

Here is a candle spell that helps call upon the power of the Sun to increase your sense of personal power. It uses a figure candle, which is a candle in the shape of a person. You can locate these online or at most new age stores.

MATERIALS

Knife or pin

Orange figure candle

Orange oil

Lighter/matches

INSTRUCTIONS

1. Carve the Sun's glyph (a circle with a dot in the center) in the figure candle's abdomen.

2. Dab a bit of orange oil on the index finger of your dominant hand and massage it into the carvings. As you do this, visualize the scenario in which you wish to have more confidence.

3. Light the candle's wick as you think about your goal or desire as you say: "Candle burning as the sun is bright, my will is strong, and power mine."

4. Focus on your personal power increasing as the candle burns. When you feel ready, blow out the flame. Relight it each day as you continue to manifest your personal power, until the candle has burned completely out.

SOLAR RETURN: A BIRTHDAY SPELL

Your birthday is also known as your solar return—the time when the Sun is in the exact same location as it was on the day you were born. This is a powerful homecoming that can be harnessed to create success for the future year. What better way to cast a solar return spell than with birthday candles? An easy way to do this and keep the number of candles at a manageable amount is by using numerology to reduce your birth age to a single digit. For instance, if you're turning 31, add the three and one to get four, the number of candles you'll use in your birthday spell. This ritual should be performed on your birthday, at the precise time of your birth (if possible), or during the Sun's planetary hour.

MATERIALS

Birthday candles in the corresponding color of your desire (see page 69)

Your favorite cake

Lighter/matches

INSTRUCTIONS

1. Hold the candles close to your heart. Close your eyes and visualize your wish for your new year.

2. Place the candles on top of the cake and light them. When you make your wish, visualize yourself attaining it.

3. Extinguish the candles with a strong but slow blow, knowing that your breath is the fuel that mixes with the transformative element of fire that is then carried by the smoke into the atmosphere to manifest.

4. Eat your cake and savor its magic.

TRANSIT MAGIC FOR THE SUN

One of the best ways to use planetary magic is by using the transits for magical timing. This is because transits are the real-life continued motion of the planets. As the celestial bodies move through space and time, their areas of influence will dominate certain positions within your natal chart, highlighting key themes. Use astrological software or apps to determine the current or future transits, then use the chart below to further enhance and develop spells or rituals that correspond to the mundane themes. For example, if the Sun is transiting through your second house, in the sign of Libra, the best spells to work include those for increasing your financial potential, harmonizing your relationships, and enhancing your personal aesthetic.

HOUSE OR SIGN	MUNDANE THEMES	MAGICAL RECOMMENDATIONS
First or Aries	Your identity, ego, and sense of self-empowerment will be in focus. Spend time connecting to what drives you in life.	Work spells for self-empowerment and overall success. Magical efforts for ambition are favorable. Burn red, orange, yellow, or gold candles. Use crystals and herbs associated with Aries.
Second or Taurus	Focus on financial power and increasing luxury.	Focus magical efforts on financial power and increasing the things you want. Burn green, gold, or silver candles with coins at the base. Use crystals and herbs associated with Taurus to energize money.
Third or Gemini	Satisfy your need to communicatively express yourself.	Use glamour magic to visually communicate who you are to the world. Wear colors that make you feel most yourself and represent how you wish to be seen. Wear an oil blend connected to Gemini.

HOUSE OR SIGN	MUNDANE THEMES	MAGICAL RECOMMENDATIONS
Fourth or Cancer	Your individuality is eclipsed by your emotions. Reflect on your emotional body and spend time doing what feels comfortable. Connect with family.	Do magic to connect with your emotions, focusing on meditation and purging emotional turmoil. Consider magic to help you stand out to your family or establish independence from them. Incorporate Cancer correspondences (e.g., herbs, crystals, sigils, etc.) into your spells and rituals.
Fifth or Leo	New opportunities for fun and creative passion present themselves. Possible stagnation in creativity may occur with unfavorable squares.	Work spells for creativity. Burn red candles to summon creativity. Work with crystals and herbs aligned with the Sun or Leo.
Sixth or Virgo	Your sense of routine will come into focus now. Attention to hard work is key. Overachieve.	Work spells for promotions or to realign focus and determination. Self-improvement is key now. Burn red or orange candles for confidence and use Virgo correspondences in spells.
Seventh or Libra	Create harmony in existing relationships and attract new ones.	Perform love and beauty spells. Burn candles or even wear shades of pink or red. Use Libra crystals and herbs.
Eighth or Scorpio	Unexpected investments are possible. Sexual performance may increase.	Practice sex magic to manifest with the energy of your orgasm. Burn red candles and focus on recharging your libido.

——→

HOUSE OR SIGN	MUNDANE THEMES	MAGICAL RECOMMENDATIONS
Ninth or Sagittarius	Increase travel or knowledge. Move outside of your comfort zone.	Read occult philosophy or learn a new aspect of magical practice. Burn candles in orange, blue, or purple during these activities and anoint with oils connected to Sagittarius.
Tenth or Capricorn	Ambitions increase, so take a lead in career aspirations.	Work road-opening spells to remove obstacles and create career opportunities. Burn candles in shades of gold. Work with other Capricorn correspondences.
Eleventh or Aquarius	Social affairs increase. Work toward establishing community. Start an organization or host an event.	Spells to attract new friends or spells of gratitude toward current friends are a good idea now. Bless local businesses and organizations with success. Burn candles in pastel shades. Incorporate Aquarius correspondences into spells and rituals, including herbs, crystals, or sigils.
Twelfth or Pisces	Focus on yourself.	Magical self-care: Take a bewitching bubble bath incorporating dried herbs or essential oils connected to Pisces to soothe your mind, body, and spirit. Burn candles in shades of pink, blue, or turquoise.

CHAPTER 6

THE MOON: EMOTIONS & COMFORT

The Moon depicts your emotional landscape. It maintains control of your emotions and routines, as well as ties to your home, ancestors, and mother figures. Many witches work with the Moon's phases and worship it as a symbol of the Goddess. It is profoundly tied to our intuition and instincts and how we nurture our sentiments astrologically. Your Moon sign, like your solar sign, plays a key role in how your Sun sign manifests itself, making it the second most important celestial body in your horoscope. This chapter focuses on using the Moon's energy in spells. At the end, you'll find an overview of magical and mundane themes to consider with the Moon's transits so you can make the most of your astrological spellcraft!

LUNAR MEDITATION

The following meditation can help you tap into the intuitive aspects of the Moon for emotional wisdom. It's best done when the Moon is in the same sign as your Moon sign, regardless of the phase, and can be done on a routine basis to realign your emotions. To track this, visit MoonCalendar.astro-seek.com.

MATERIALS

Mugwort tea

Laptop or smartphone (optional)

Cushion or yoga mat to sit on

Lighter/matches

Lavender incense and lighter/ matches

Lavender oil

Journal and pen

INSTRUCTIONS

1. Brew a cup of mugwort tea. Pour it into a cup and find a comfortable and silent place.

2. Play the ASMR/white noise audio of Moon sounds found in my public Planetary Magic Meditation playlist on YouTube (see Resources on page 174) to focus your meditation and call upon the Moon's energy.

3. Sit in a relaxed stance. Light the incense and fan the smoke in your direction. Apply a small amount of oil to your wrists and clavicle.

4. Take a sip of your tea. Close your eyes and breathe deeply through your nose for 10 seconds before slowly exhaling through your mouth.

5. Visualize the Moon in its fullness, suspended in the sky and glowing brightly. Focus on your emotional landscape. Reflect on the following: What am I feeling right now? What doesn't seem to be working for me? What has shown to be effective for me? What do I require? What do I take pride in? What am I able to let go of?

6. Remain in the meditative state for at least 30 minutes before you slowly come back to full consciousness. Record any revelations in your journal.

TAROT SPREAD FOR INTUITIVE GUIDANCE

The new moon and the full moon are prominent times for witches to work with divination tools to forecast their future. Here is my take on the traditional Celtic Cross spread, which is one of the most popular among readers.

MATERIALS

Mugwort tea

Incense blend of equal parts cinnamon, myrrh, and sandalwood

4 white candles

Amethyst, labradorite, or selenite crystals

Tarot deck

Journal and pen

INSTRUCTIONS

1. Drink mugwort tea while burning the incense, along with four white candles to assist you in your reading. If you have them, amethyst, labradorite, or selenite crystals can be worn or placed alongside the cards to further stimulate the psychic connection.

2. Close your eyes and shuffle the cards. As you do, ask the moon to guide you and show you what you need to know at this moment. Draw the cards in the following pattern and use the key below to decipher their meaning. Record your findings in your journal.

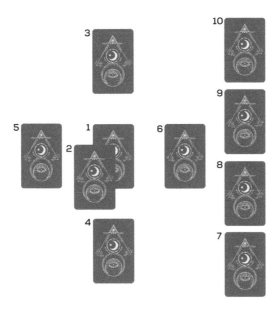

- **Querent (1):** The present energy surrounding you

- **Cross Card (2):** The reason for or roadblock concerning your current situation

- **Known Influences (3):** That of which you are currently aware

- **Unknown Influences (4):** The subconscious factors of which you are unaware

- **Past Influences (5):** The past events contributing to the present situation

- **Near Future (6):** The situation's likely result in the near future

- **Your Thoughts (7):** How you feel about your situation

- **Other People's Thoughts (8):** How others are affecting or seeing you

- **Hope or Anxieties (9):** Your hopes or fears about the situation, depending on the energy of the card chosen

- **Overall Outcome (10):** The underlying message that the person should consider

FULL MOON RITUAL OF GRATITUDE

The Moon is associated with not only our feelings and intuition but also our memories. A powerful aspect of magic is giving thanks for the blessings and obstacles that have created growth in your life. Rituals of gratitude are powerful, as they help magnetize your future intentions with the universe so that it can bring more greatness your way. This is a full moon ritual of gratitude to reflect upon all for which you are thankful.

MATERIALS

Paper

Pen

Crystal or glass bowl

Clear quartz obelisk (a crystal that when standing has a point facing upward)

Spring water (enough to fill the bowl halfway)

A fresh, beautiful white flower in bloom (e.g., gardenia, orchid, peony, or rose)

INSTRUCTIONS

1. Find a place that will not be easily disturbed in a windowsill or outside during a full moon. Gaze at the Moon and reflect upon all for which you are grateful. Make a list.

2. Set the list on a flat surface. Place the bowl on top of it, with the crystal directly in the center to anchor the energy of your gratitude.

3. Pour the water into the bowl as a symbolic reference to the emotional body of water inside of you.

4. Place the white flower in the water so that it floats with the Moon's rays falling upon it. Gaze into the lunar orb and speak from your heart, expressing your gratitude.

5. Leave the flower floating in the Moon's light. The next day, pour the water onto the land and dry your flower on your altar. Once completely dried, separate the petals and blow them in the wind as an offering to the universe.

EMOTIONAL WATERS BATHING RITUAL

Because of the relationship between the Moon and tides, bathing during the night of a full moon can be profoundly magical. Look at baths as one big cauldron, in which you get to be one of the ingredients. Considering the elemental correspondences of water, it is also deeply tied to emotions, making bath magic a way to cope with your emotions.

MATERIALS

1 single fresh white rose
1 tablespoon Epsom salt
5 drops lavender essential oil

Mixing bowl
Lighter/matches
Light blue candle

INSTRUCTIONS

1. Pull the petals off the white rose and combine them with Epsom salt and 5 drops of essential oil in a mixing bowl.

2. Think about your emotions. Are you feeling overly sensitive? Stoic? Is there something troubling you? Focus on this as you stir in a clockwise motion.

3. Fill a bath with warm water and toss in the petals with the salt and oil mixture.

4. Turn off the lights and light the candle, which you should place near the bath.

5. Soak for 20 minutes in the water. Continue to fixate on your emotional landscape. As you do so, allow the calming waters to soothe you.

6. Rinse, dry, and take the remaining rose petals outside. Toss them above you and offer them to the Moon for emotional healing.

TRANSIT MAGIC FOR THE MOON

Use the following chart to further enhance or develop your astrological Moon magic. Use astrological software or apps to determine the current or future transits of the Moon and create spells or rituals that correspond to the themes outlined below. For example, if the Moon is transiting through your sixth house in the sign of Pisces, the best spells to work include self-care to balance daily routines or enhance intuition.

HOUSE OR SIGN	MUNDANE THEMES	MAGICAL RECOMMENDATIONS
First or Aries	Explore emotional connection toward appearance and identity. Now is the time to change things up and express yourself through your appearance.	Cast glamour spells or give yourself a magical makeover. Wear the colors that correspond with what you wish to manifest, and mix fragrance oils that enhance identity or are fueled by Aries energy.
Second or Taurus	Emotional needs for possessions and security come into focus. Avoid binge shopping to cope with stress.	Cast spells for comfort and security. Purify and cleanse your house by burning brown, green, or pink candles brushed with mica and anointed with Taurean oils to enhance your home with luxurious energy.
Third or Gemini	Emotional communication comes to the forefront. Freely speak from your heart. On the flip side, be patient during times of frustration to avoid emotionally lashing out or being overly sensitive.	Perform magic that allows you to express your emotional needs. Burn candles that are light blue, white, or silver. Burn incense or make oils connected to Gemini. Meditate while lying down, with a piece of celestite resting on your neck to strengthen your throat chakra.

HOUSE OR SIGN	MUNDANE THEMES	MAGICAL RECOMMENDATIONS
Fourth or Cancer	Establish emotional connection to family and homelife. Maternal instincts are at a high. Get your homelife in order.	Perform spells or rituals that strengthen your bond with members of your family. Alternatively, bless your home.
Fifth or Leo	You have an emotional connection with pleasure. Love and sex are highlighted. Emotional creativity and inspiration waxes or wanes depending on squares.	Self-love spells and sex magic are good ways to tap into your source for personal pleasure. Reflect on your passions and desires while utilizing Leo energy. Candle and fire magic is also powerful at this time.
Sixth or Virgo	Your sense of routine will be emotionally charged. This may affect work or homelife. There are sensitivities with coworkers and housemates. Emotions may affect health.	Practice self-care rituals to realign your mind, body, and spirit. Practice rituals of meditation or bath magic to recharge, rest, and comfort emotional strains. Remember that to serve, you have to care for yourself first.
Seventh or Libra	Emotional connections to partnership, bringing closeness (or distance if squared in an adversarial way) between you and others, come into play.	This is a good time for love spells, or spells that bring justice to emotional traumas. Use shades of pink with Libra correspondences to establish harmony.
Eighth or Scorpio	Emotionally charged connection to shared money and intimate sexual situations come into focus. Your intuition will be in overdrive; trust it as you navigate daily life.	Burn black candles to absorb negative emotions connected to finances or sex. Practice sex magic to emotionally connect with your sensual side. Intuitive work can help you uncover unseen truths.

HOUSE OR SIGN	MUNDANE THEMES	MAGICAL RECOMMENDATIONS
Ninth or Sagittarius	A need to learn or try something new will be heightened. Travel for inspiration or educating yourself in a new philosophy or process is best now.	Spells or rituals related to movement are best now. Practice magic to establish freedom from confines and explore new ideas.
Tenth or Capricorn	Sensitivities to how you are seen come to light.	Cast spells to enhance public appearance. Spells to gain emotional recognition or validation are best practiced now. Make a list of career goals and burn the petition to manifest success.
Eleventh or Aquarius	Emotional connection to social settings will heighten. Spend time with friends, supporting social causes you are emotionally invested in, or give back to local businesses.	Cast spells in favor of local businesses or community events. Practice rituals of gratitude for the friendships you have. Use Aquarius correspondences in magical efforts.
Twelfth or Pisces	A deep connection to your subconscious emotions comes into focus. Pay attention to your sense of spirituality.	Psychic work is good now to tap further into your intuition. Sleep with labradorite under your pillow to help enhance psychic abilities. Use purple candles and Pisces correspondences.

CHAPTER 7

MERCURY: COMMUNICATION & MIND

Mercury is the master of the tongue and mind, influencing our thoughts, speech, and comprehension. It can also tell you how focused you are and how to handle distractions better. Plus, it can shed light on intellectual curiosity and social relations, depending on the placement of your Mercury sign, and things like your wit, fears, and concerns. Mercurial energy may help you become more adaptive to conditions in your life, as well. This chapter focuses on using mercurial energy in spells. At the end, you'll find an overview of magical and mundane themes to consider with Mercury's transits so that you can make the most of your astrological spellcraft!

MERCURIAL MEDITATION

The following meditation is designed to help you tap into Mercury's powers of mental prowess and communication.

MATERIALS

Peppermint tea

Laptop or smartphone
  (optional)

Cushion or yoga mat to sit on

Lighter/matches

Mint incense

Mint oil

Journal and pen

INSTRUCTIONS

1. Make a cup of peppermint tea and bring it to a comfortable and quiet place.

2. Play the ASMR/white noise Mercury audio found in my public Planetary Magic Meditation playlist on YouTube (see Resources on page 174) to help stimulate your meditation and focus on Mercury's energy.

3. Sit in a relaxed stance. Light the incense and fan the smoke in your direction. Apply a dab of oil to your wrists and clavicle.

4. Close your eyes as you enjoy your tea and breathe deeply through your nose for 10 seconds before slowly exhaling through your mouth.

5. Visualize the planet Mercury as you reflect on the following: How do I express myself verbally and nonverbally? In what ways can I better express my wants and needs? How can I be a better listener and in what ways will that benefit me? How do I react to criticism—constructively or destructively? How do I make decisions? Slow, fast, strategically? How can I flex this? What is my personal truth?

6. Remain in the meditative state for at least 30 minutes before you slowly come back to consciousness. Record any revelations in your journal.

REVERSE BAD COMMUNICATION

Following is a simple spell to ease tension during negative communication. It is a great spell to perform in preparation of Mercury retrograde, a time when communication tends to go awry. Perform this spell on Wednesday during the planetary hour of Mercury. If doing the spell for the retrograde, do it the Wednesday before the retrograde begins.

MATERIALS

Yellow chime candle and holder

Knife

Oil blend (equal parts lavender, lemongrass, and vetiver)

Herbal blend (equal parts dried lavender, lemongrass, and vetiver)

Lighter/matches

INSTRUCTIONS

1. Turn the yellow candle upside down and chip away at the wax at the end until the wick is exposed. You will be lighting the candle from the opposite end to represent the reversal of bad communication.

2. Carve the symbol for Mercury on one side of the candle and your name (initials are okay if your name is long) on the other. Lick your thumb and trace your saliva over your name to create an energetic bond.

3. Dress your candle with oil and roll it in your ground herbal blend. Place it in the holder and light the exposed wick while saying: *"May communication be a breeze, our thoughts and words flow with ease."*

4. Focus intently on the area of your life that lacks clear communication and how you wish for it to smooth out.

5. Allow the candle to burn out completely. Continue to chant the above incantation when faced with a communication mishap.

TO MAKE A DECISION

Mercury's energy can help when you are stuck and not sure which decision to make. Many witches will use divination to sort out the most favorable action. Here is a simple way to pair Mercury's energy with a pendulum for decision making.

MATERIALS

Salt   Pendulum

INSTRUCTIONS

1. Make a flat circle of salt on a level surface.

2. Use your finger to draw a vertical line through the circle, splitting it in half.

3. Decide which half of the circle represents a yes and which a no response. You may wish to write this in the salt pile itself if you prefer.

4. Close your eyes and hold the pendulum over the salt. Keep the pendulum stable when asking a question; it will move seemingly on its own in response. Pay attention to the movements when you ask the question and concentrate on it.

If this is your first time using a pendulum, it might be better to start by asking yes or no questions to which you already know the answers.

SAFE TRAVELS AMULET

Mercury is not only the planet of communication, but also a planet connected to travel. This simple spell involves creating a magical object to help protect you on your travels.

MATERIALS

1 bay leaf

3 black peppercorns

Piece black tourmaline (to ward away trouble)

Piece aquamarine (for safety and emotions)

Yellow drawstring pouch

2 iron nails

Piece light blue thread the length of your foot

INSTRUCTIONS

1. Place the bay leaf, peppercorns, and crystals into the yellow pouch.

2. Cross the iron nails together and tie them into place with the light blue thread. Iron is known for repelling negativity, and light blue is associated with tranquility and protection. The cross pattern helps establish stability.

3. Tie the bag closed. Hold the pouch close to your heart. Close your eyes and call upon Mercury to bless your travel plans with these words: "I call on the powers of Mercury to assist with my travel safety. Help me get from point A to B with your protection and power, swiftly!"

4. Visualize your travel plans and safely reaching your destination with ease.

5. Carry the amulet with you during travel. If you drive, hang the amulet inside the car. If traveling by plane, be sure to place in checked luggage to avoid issues with security.

TRANSIT MAGIC FOR MERCURY

The following chart can be used to further enhance or develop your astrological magic with Mercury. Use astrological software or apps to determine the current or future transits of Mercury and create spells or rituals that correspond to the mundane themes outlined below.

HOUSE OR SIGN	MUNDANE THEMES	MAGICAL RECOMMENDATIONS
First or Aries	New ideas come freely; however, your communication may be aggressive and pushy.	Cast spells to enhance imagination and creativity or to soften your communication style and minimize friction. Use cool colors to balance the fiery nature of this sign/house.
Second or Taurus	Thinking may become slower and more methodical. Your decisions will be fixed and unchangeable. Focus on money and possessions.	Drink tea made from orange peel to stir up stagnant energy and help open the mind to new decisions. Burn orange candles for energy. Also, this is a good time for money spells.
Third or Gemini	This is one of the best Mercury placements. Your mind is active and engaged. You're quick-witted with a sharp tongue and easily able to communicate and share knowledge.	Use yellow and blue in magical efforts to stimulate mental imagination and effortless speech. Now is the time to say what you need to say. Wear necklaces of lapis, amazonite, or turquoise to open the throat chakra. Wear mint ChapStick or lip gloss to communicate well.
Fourth or Cancer	Your communication style will be anchored in sensitivity. You may come off as needy, naggy, or overly emotional at this time.	Spells to promote comfort, calmness, and tranquility are recommended. Burn white candles, lavender, or gardenia incense. Spend time in water; bath magic is perfect.

HOUSE OR SIGN	MUNDANE THEMES	MAGICAL RECOMMENDATIONS
Fifth or Leo	You communicate through performance. You may be feeling an urge to be "extra" and express yourself in a grand way.	Play with glamour and beauty spells to communicate your inner narrative with external presence. Enchant your outfits with cinnamon incense. Get ready surrounded in red, orange, and yellow candles. Change up your appearance in a big, bold way.
Sixth or Virgo	Mercury is at home here. Your thoughts will be fixated on improvements and perfection. Be careful not to push others away with harsh or judgmental communication styles.	Now is a great time to focus on your goals and aspirations. Make a list of desired improvements and burn them in a cauldron. Be sure to hold yourself accountable with real-life action.
Seventh or Libra	Positive and diplomatic communication will take place as your mind fixates on partnerships and harmonizing interactions with others.	Love and friendship spells are a good idea now. So are spells to bond with coworkers and peers. Use lavender in spells. Burn light pink candles.
Eighth or Scorpio	You may feel psychically sensitive now, with a keen ability to see through bullshit. Emotions can cause anger and frustrative outbursts.	Wear black and burn black candles to repel negative thoughts. Enhance your intuition and soothe your emotions by carrying or wearing amethyst.
Ninth or Sagittarius	Your thoughts will be focused on expansion and learning new things. In your quest for finding truth and learning new things, be careful not to come off as dogmatic or preachy.	Expand your witchy knowledge by reading and researching different areas of the occult to incorporate into your practice. Spells for knowledge and wisdom are good now. Work with shades of yellow and purple.

→

HOUSE OR SIGN	MUNDANE THEMES	MAGICAL RECOMMENDATIONS
Tenth or Capricorn	An emphasis on public perception is in order now. Opportunities for public speaking and presentations may pop up. Pay attention to your public image.	Work spells to communicate your legacy. Witchy writing is a good idea now, so work on crafting your book of shadows, writing blogs, and/ or working on books.
Eleventh or Aquarius	Technological communication and community are highlighted. Be mindful of your social media presence.	Design a sigil or power symbol that is anchored in your spiritual truth. Lower the opacity using photo software and overlay it onto a photo of yourself. Share it on social media as an act of online witchery.
Twelfth or Pisces	Creative communication is the focus now. Thoughts will be imaginative and artistic.	Make a vision board using only words to convey your wishes and desires. Place it on your altar to amplify your creation.

CHAPTER 8

VENUS: LOVE & RELATIONSHIPS

Named after the Roman goddess of love, Venus oversees attachment, both to material resources and emotional partnerships. This planet is known for its unusual orbit, which creates a five-petaled flower in the sky. Venus has been considered the witch's star because this fivefold image closely resembles a pentagram—the symbol of witchcraft. The flower shape also connects Venus's energy to concepts of beauty like the arts, luxury, and sensualism. Your Venus sign placement will determine how you prefer to give and receive love, work in partnerships, and relate to material means. At the end, you'll find an overview of magical and mundane themes to consider with Venus's transits so that you can make the most of your astrological spellcraft!

VENUSIAN MEDITATION

This meditation is designed for you to tap into all things Venus—love, beauty, pleasure, and sensuality. Perform it on a Friday or during the hour of Venus.

MATERIALS

Hibiscus or rose tea

Laptop or smartphone
  (optional)

Cushion or yoga mat to sit on

Lighter/matches

Rose incense

Rose oil

Journal and pen

INSTRUCTIONS

1. Make a cup of tea, and sit somewhere quiet and comfy.

2. Play the ASMR/white noise audio of Venus sounds from my public Planetary Magic Meditation playlist on YouTube (see Resources on page 174).

3. Sit in a comfortable position. Light the incense and direct the smoke your way. Apply a dab of oil on your wrists and clavicle.

4. Close your eyes as you drink the tea. Breathe deeply through your nose for 10 seconds before slowly exhaling through your mouth.

5. Visualize the bright planet of Venus while focusing on your heartbeat as you reflect on the following: How do I feel about love? How do I express love and how do I want to be loved? Who do I love and who currently loves me? What makes me feel sensual? What makes me feel attractive? How can I better express love and beauty in the world?

6. Remain in the meditative state for at least 30 minutes before you slowly come back to consciousness. Record any revelations in your journal.

TO CONJURE A NEW LOVE

This is for all the single witches out there looking to find a new love. While love spells can be a taboo practice, the best kind involves drawing your ideal lover to you of their own free will. It is best to perform this spell during the planetary hour of Venus, seven days before the full moon.

MATERIALS

Paper

Pen

Plate

Knife

2 pink figure candles

Lemon oil

Sugar

1 rose quartz

Lighters/match

Pink rose

Pink drawstring pouch

INSTRUCTIONS

1. Write down a list of all the qualities you long for in a lover. When finished, kiss the paper with love.

2. Place the list on a level surface with the plate on top of it.

3. Carve your name into the figure candle that represents you, along with the symbols of your Sun, Moon, and Venus signs. Carve any astrological signs that would be compatible with your natal chart into the other candle. Anoint each with the lemon oil and rub them down with sugar.

4. Place each candle on the plate so they are facing each other with the crystal between them.

5. Light the candles and pick up the rose. Create a heart shape around the candles by pulling one petal off at a time, chanting: "By the flame of Venus, I conjure thee, I call love to me."

continued

6. Gaze into the flames and visualize the perfect partner coming into your life.

7. Extinguish the candles. Relight, chant, and visualize your ideal partner on the day or the hour of Venus until the night of the full moon. Then, allow the remaining candle to burn completely out. Place the wax remains, list, crystal, and rose petals in the pink pouch. Carry your love talisman with you. Your love will find you.

CRYSTAL GRID FOR LOVE & HARMONY

A crystal grid is a collection of different crystals arranged in a geometric pattern to aid in the manifestation of desired outcomes. Here is a grid template to help create harmony and fill your space with Venus's loving energy.

MATERIALS

1 heart-shaped rose quartz
3 tumbled pieces emerald
3 tumbled pieces rhodonite

6 clear quartz points
Lighter/matches
Rose incense stick

INSTRUCTIONS

1. Find a level space in your home to create your grid. Be sure that it is somewhere that will not be disturbed by roommates, children, or pets.

2. Place the rose quartz heart in the center of the space. The grid will be formed using a hexagram consisting of two opposing triangles. This six-pointed shape helps instill harmony and balance.

3. Alternate placing the emerald and rhodonite pieces at the intersecting points in the middle of the shape.

4. Place the clear quartz crystal points at each outer point of the hexagram, with the points facing outward.

5. Bless and activate the grid by lighting the stick of incense and tracing the smoke over the shape while calling upon Venus: "Venus, planet of love, may you bless my home and space with love, harmony, balance, and grace."

6. Visualize your heart lighting up with a glowing pink light as you chant the line above.

7. Allow the incense to burn out. Revisit the grid when you need a boost of love, compassion, or harmony.

VENUSIAN NIGHT ENCHANTMENT

Cast this spell to make an entry with enchanting beauty. Wear luxurious clothing for this spell, preferably something bright and flashy, though head-to-toe black will work well, too. Accessorize with elegant jewelry. This spell is perfect to perform in preparation for a date or on a Friday night out with friends.

MATERIALS

Body glitter (optional)

Outfit and jewelry of choice

Knife

2 green candles

2 pink candles

Cinnamon oil

Rose oil

Gold or silver mica

Lighter/matches

INSTRUCTIONS

1. Prepare for your evening as you normally would: Bathe/shower, groom, do your hair and makeup, etc. Add a dash of body glitter if you feel inclined for some extra sparkle.

2. Dress yourself slowly while envisioning yourself as the ultimate enchanter.

3. Carve the symbol of Venus into each of the candles and anoint them with one drop of oil. Sprinkle the candles with a bit of mica for some glamorous sparkle.

4. Create a circle with the candles on the floor. Stand in the center and light the candles in a clockwise direction. Invoke the blessings of Venus for a glamorous night out: "I am full of glamour and full of grace. Enchanting those who see my face. May I radiate Venusian light and transfix everyone with my sight."

5. Visualize yourself as the supreme vision of beauty and glamour in the universe. Blow out the candles one by one and step into the night for bewitching fun!

TRANSIT MAGIC FOR VENUS

The chart below can be used to further enhance or develop your astrological magic with Venus. Use astrological software or apps to determine the current or future transits of Venus and create spells or rituals that correspond to the themes outlined below.

HOUSE OR SIGN	MUNDANE THEMES	MAGICAL RECOMMENDATIONS
First or Aries	An emphasis on beauty and appearance in in store. Aspects of love in your life will be filled with passion and vitality.	Wear shades of red or hot pink to call upon personal power and flirtation. Spicy fragrances will help create a bold allure.
Second or Taurus	A strong fixation on the sensual—taste, smells, touch, sight, and sounds—will bring comfort.	Create a spiritual spa day perfect for a magical makeover. Use witchcraft lotions, potions, and other attraction-based infusions. Self-love spells are a good idea now.
Third or Gemini	Words will come easily now as your thoughts and communication flow with romanticism.	Do some witchy writing now—poetry, blog postings, or even an article for submission. Write passionately about an area in your practice that is important to you.
Fourth or Cancer	Love in connection to your home will be highlighted. This could indicate a strong connection to family, especially mother, or those with whom you live. At the same time, your home becomes the center of attention for beauty and pleasure.	Use a bit of beauty magic in your home. Make a rosewater wash and clean the surfaces of your home to open it up to all acts of love and pleasure. Place fresh-cut, pet-safe flowers around the home, and put pieces of rose quartz in the soil of houseplants. Love spells to harmonize family relations are a good idea now.

HOUSE OR SIGN	MUNDANE THEMES	MAGICAL RECOMMENDATIONS
Fifth or Leo	This transit can be a potent time for meeting new love interests. Here, aspects of love and beauty make a big splash. Have fun and attract the love you want into your life now.	Focus your magical efforts now on attracting new love or exploring new facets of love. Come to me love spells are highly effective. Use color magic in makeup and clothing to further raise energy in all spellcasting.
Sixth or Virgo	Love will enter the world of your daily routine. This is a good time to bond with coworkers or peers.	Create a harmonizing room spray to use in work or school environments by combining 2.5 ounces distilled water, 0.25 ounce alcohol, 10 drops of rose oil, 10 drops of lavender oil, and five drops of lemon oil into a 4-ounce spray bottle. Add a tumbled amethyst and rose quartz, too.
Seventh or Libra	Romance and partnership are key now. Beauty and harmony are driving factors in your life.	Love spells in general are especially powerful now. Burn pink candles and use roses in magical workings to instill harmony and bliss. Work with loving crystals like rose quartz, pink tourmaline, rhodochrosite, and rhodonite.
Eighth or Scorpio	Sexual love will be empha-sized, as will deep-rooted commitments that you exchange with others.	Cast spells to enhance the pleasure of lovemaking. Use red or pink candles in the bedroom. Burn rose incense. Massage oils infused with essential oils can enhance your magic.

HOUSE OR SIGN	MUNDANE THEMES	MAGICAL RECOMMENDATIONS
Ninth or Sagittarius	Aspects of love from afar will come into play. This is a good time for romantic getaways or traveling to find love.	Get lost in supernatural love stories. Find inspiration in a witchy love story and use it as inspiration for real-life spellcraft. Also, this is a good time to anchor your love in spirituality and magic to establish harmony.
Tenth or Capricorn	Your public perception will be enhanced by aspects of love. It's a good time to highlight your best qualities in the workplace to receive validation and admiration.	Make a mirror wash to gain public love. Boil a mixture of petals from three orange roses, one orange peel, scrapings from one vanilla bean, and 1 teaspoon of powdered cinnamon. Strain, cool, and bottle the mixture. Smear it on mirrors and reflective surfaces in public.
Eleventh or Aquarius	Your social situations will blossom.	This is a great time to do spells to attract new friends or harmonize and strengthen the bonds of existing friendships. Make friendship bracelets using beaded crystals to harmonize your bond.
Twelfth or Pisces	Romanticizing the imaginary is highlighted at this time. Intense daydreaming will pull you away from the mundane world.	Place rose quartz, rhodochrosite, or rhodonite under your pillow to dream of your true love.

CHAPTER 9

MARS: ACTION & DESIRE

Mars is named after the Roman god of war. It is a planet anchored in action and movement. Because of its godly characterization, it also exudes aggression, and natal Mars placements indicate how we deal with adversarial conflict. At the same time, it is steeped in carnal passions and sexual desire. A determined planet, its energy is a source of inner and physical strength, mixed with aspects of independence and high bursts of energy. Tap into its energy when choosing what battles to fight, seeking an energy boost, or enhancing your sex life. This chapter includes a handful of spells and rituals anchored in this mighty planet's vigor. There's also an overview of themes to consider during Mars's transits for you to maximize your astrological spellcraft!

MARTIAN MEDITATION

The following meditation is designed for you to contemplate the powerful, courageous, and sensual powers of Mars.

MATERIALS

Rooibos tea

Laptop or smartphone
 (optional)

Cushion or yoga mat to sit on

Lighter/matches

Lavender incense

Lavender oil

Journal and pen

INSTRUCTIONS

1. Brew and pour yourself a cup of rooibos tea. Find a comfortable and silent place to relax.

2. Play the ASMR/white noise audio found in my public Planetary Magic Meditation playlist on YouTube (see Resources on page 174) to help stimulate your meditation and focus on Mars's energy.

3. Get into a comfortable and relaxed position. Light the incense and fan the smoke in your direction. Apply a small amount of oil to your wrists and clavicle.

4. Sip your tea and close your eyes. Breathe deeply through your nose for 10 seconds before slowly exhaling through your mouth.

5. Visualize Mars and reflect on the following: What is my personal power? Am I ambitious? How can I be more proactive? In what ways have I been brave and strong? What have I endured? How can I be more independent and courageous? How do I express and nurture my sexuality? What excites me and feeds my personal pleasure center?

6. Remain in this meditative state for at least 30 minutes before you slowly come back to consciousness. Record any revelations in your journal.

A CALL FOR ACTION

Whether you are seeking motivation to move forward or to speed a situation along, this spell is designed to call upon Mars for action and speedy results.

MATERIALS

Parchment paper
Red pen
Lighter or match

Cauldron or fireproof dish
Ground allspice

INSTRUCTIONS

1. Write your name on the paper in three rows.

2. Turn the page so that you can now write the word "action" in three rows over your name so that it crosses your previous writings.

3. Turn the page in a clockwise direction and write down what you desire.

4. Use a lighter or match to light your petition on fire and place it in the cauldron or dish.

5. Add a sprinkle of allspice to the flames and say this incantation as it burns: "I call upon the power of Mars to bring action to (your desire). May swift and speedy results manifest for me."

6. As your words burn and turn to smoke, your desires are released into the universe. Allow the embers to die and cauldron or dish to cool. Toss the ashes into the wind. Your desired action will manifest swiftly.

COURAGE OIL

This oil recipe combines oils that are associated with Mars to summon fiery courage.

MATERIALS

12 drops ginger oil

10 drops basil oil

5 drops black pepper oil

1 (15-milliliter) roller ball bottle

Fractionated coconut oil

1 small piece High John the Conqueror root

Knife

INSTRUCTIONS

1. Add the ginger oil, basil oil, and black pepper oil, one by one, to the roller ball bottle. Focus on the courageous powers of Mars as you do so.

2. Add as much fractionated coconut oil as needed to fill the remaining space in the bottle.

3. Enchant the High John root by saying: "I call on the strength of Mars—courage and power—to conquer my challenges and fear."

4. Break a piece of the root or use the knife to shave a bit into the bottle. Cap the bottle and shake it vigorously as you visualize yourself acting courageously.

5. Wear the mixture topically on your body to summon courage or anoint spell items, such as candles, bags, etc.

COME TO ME LUST SPELL

Whether you are single or partnered, this spell is designed to summon sensuality and spice up your sex life. Perform it on a Tuesday night during the hour of Mars.

MATERIALS

Red pen

Parchment paper

1 red candle with 7 hours of burn time

Lust oil blend (1 part musk oil, 1 part rose oil, and 1 part black pepper oil)

Lust powder (1 tbsp. dragon's blood powder, 1 tbsp. allspice; and 1 tbsp. cayenne pepper)

1 red rose in vase

Lighter/matches

Red drawstring bag

INSTRUCTIONS

1. Write a letter of lust and passion in red pen on the parchment paper, emphasizing all the sensual, spicy things you would like to do with your lover.

2. Anoint the candle with the three drops of the lust oil and a pinch of lust powder.

3. Place the candle on top of your letter with the rose in vase. Sprinkle the powder around the candle and vase in a clockwise direction as you chant "Come to me" over and over.

4. Light the candle's wick and say: "I ignite the flame of lust within me—enhancing my sexuality. May my nights be filled with passion and ecstasy."

5. Focus and visualize your perfect steamy night. After about an hour, blow a kiss to the flame to extinguish the light.

6. For the next six nights, reapply the oil and a pinch of powder to the candle and relight the wick during the hour of Mars. Once the candle has completely burned out, add any magical remains, including any remaining powder and the withered rose petals, to the drawstring bag. Place it under your mattress. Lust will manifest.

TRANSIT MAGIC FOR MARS

Use the chart below to further enhance or develop your astrological magic with Mars. Use astrological software or apps to determine the current or future transits of Mars and create spells or rituals that correspond to the themes outlined below.

HOUSE OR SIGN	MUNDANE THEMES	MAGICAL RECOMMENDATIONS
First or Aries	Mars is at home here. Ambition and aggression kick into overdrive.	Anchor magical goals in your passions. Write these on a piece of paper and burn them with the transformative power of fire. Combat aggression with candlelit baths infused with lavender, chamomile, orange, sandalwood, or clary sage.
Second or Taurus	Your attitude toward money and luxury will be ambitious. Conflict over money or spending habits is likely. Unexpected spending may occur.	Prosperity spells are advised now. Wear jewelry or carry pieces of pyrite to stimulate financial gain and protect you from adversarial situations.
Third or Gemini	Your communication will be assertive but may come off as aggressive.	Practice spells for easy communication and minimize conflict.
Fourth or Cancer	Homelife may experience tension and frustration.	Make an incense blend of cinnamon, orange peel, and vanilla bean powder to restore lost energy and stimulate happiness in your home.
Fifth or Leo	Physical pleasure takes the forefront of your focus.	Spells to spice up your sex life are a good idea, as are spells to energize and recharge your physical body.

HOUSE OR SIGN	MUNDANE THEMES	MAGICAL RECOMMENDATIONS
Sixth or Virgo	This is a good time for organization and getting things done. Work and routines will be easier. Physical activity may increase.	Wear shades of orange or red when working out or engaging in physical activity to stimulate stamina.
Seventh or Libra	Creative differences may create disharmony in partnerships. Disagreements on all accounts will be highlighted.	Work spells for boundaries to minimize conflict in partnerships of all kinds.
Eighth or Scorpio	You may have strong and aggressive reactions during this time, especially about secrets or miscommunications. Jealousy is also a theme now.	Protective magic is advised now. Work with black candles to banish negativity and red to draw upon power and passion. Burn dragon's blood incense.
Ninth or Sagittarius	You wish to share your philosophies as truths now. Remain open-minded and try not to project while sharing.	Reflect on your spiritual goals and disciplines. What does being a witch mean to you? Work on creating your own set of ethics and philosophies and why these are important to you. Document them in your Book of Shadows.
Tenth or Capricorn	Conflicts in career and frustration may occur now, driven by ambition and a need to succeed.	Enhance your career path with Mars's ambition by creating a résumé for the future with the job titles and responsibilities you want over time. Burn the résumé and scatter the ashes in the wind.

$\longrightarrow$

HOUSE OR SIGN	MUNDANE THEMES	MAGICAL RECOMMENDATIONS
Eleventh or Aquarius	Your social life is invigorated. Be careful not to spread yourself too thin.	Create a crystal grid using fluorite and clear quartz. Charge your day planner or phone in the grid to bring focus and order to your social calendar and schedule.
Twelfth or Pisces	Secrets are energized by Mars's fiery energy. Don't overshare what you are planning now.	Do magic to guard yourself and your goals from haters. Protection magic of all kinds is recommended now.

CHAPTER 10

JUPITER: ABUNDANCE & SUCCESS

The largest planet of the solar system, Jupiter was named after the Roman king of the gods. Because of its size, it is often associated with expansion and growth and providing opportunities to achieve such. Jupiter is a road opener. It is also the first of the outer planets, giving it a connection to group settings. Jupiter placements in a natal chart will showcase how good fortune presents itself to you, in addition to aspects of adventure, travel, and even how education may play a part in the opportunities that present themselves to you. This chapter focuses on using Jupiter's energy for astrological magic. A handful of spells and rituals inspired by this giant planet's energy are followed by an overview of themes for Jupiter's transits.

JUPITER MEDITATION

The following meditation is designed to help you tap into Jupiter's spiritual powers of growth and abundance.

MATERIALS

Dandelion tea

Laptop or smartphone
  (optional)

Cushion or yoga mat to sit on

Lighter/matches

Sage incense

Cinnamon or clove oil (diluted)

Journal and pen

INSTRUCTIONS

1. Brew a cup of dandelion tea, and find a comfortable and silent place to sit.

2. Play the ASMR/white noise audio of Jupiter sounds found in my public Planetary Magic Meditation playlist on YouTube (see Resources on page 174) to focus on the planet's energy and put you in a meditative state.

3. Sit in a relaxed stance. Light the incense and fan the smoke in your direction. Apply a small amount of oil to your wrists and clavicle.

4. Take a sip of your tea. Close your eyes and breathe deeply through your nose for 10 seconds before slowly exhaling through your mouth.

5. Visualize the planet Jupiter while reflecting on the following: What are my biggest accomplishments? How have I grown and where do I want to go next? What is my big vision and how can I get started? What obstacles stand in the way and how can I overcome them? How is my money being spent? What resources do I need to succeed?

6. Remain in the meditative state for at least 30 minutes before you slowly come back to consciousness. Record any revelations in your journal.

ROAD-OPENING CHARM

Here is a spell to unlock opportunity within your life. It is best performed during the planetary hour of Jupiter on a Thursday.

MATERIALS

Salt

4 candleholders

Skeleton key or key charm

4 green chime candles

Clove oil

Gold mica

Lighter/matches

INSTRUCTIONS

1. Create a ring of salt on a level surface. Place the candleholders at each of the cardinal points of the circle.

2. Use the key to carve the glyph of Jupiter into the wax of each candle, along with the word "OPEN." Lick your thumb and trace your saliva into each carving to bind to your energy.

3. Anoint the candles with a drop or two of the oil.

4. Sprinkle a pinch of mica on each candle and further massage it all over the wax. Place each candle into the holders.

5. Place the key in the center of the circle. Light the wick of each candle in a clockwise direction.

6. Use your index finger of your dominant hand to push a line through the salt between each candle, creating an opening. Start in the space between north and east and move in a clockwise direction while chanting: "From north to east, south to west, open the road that is the best."

7. Visualize success coming your way. Allow the candles to burn completely out. Carry the key with you each day. Doors will begin opening for you.

MONEY SPELL

Here is a simple and effective money spell. For best results, perform it on a Thursday during the planetary hour of Jupiter.

MATERIALS

Paper

Pen

Knife or pin

Green candle

Mint oil

INSTRUCTIONS

1. Make a list of your financial goals on paper, being realistic. Instead of saying you want to win the lottery, say something like "I want to be valued more at work so that I can obtain a raise" or "I'd like to treat the money that comes into my life with greater care so that I'm not as wasteful with it."

2. Carve your name on one side of the candle and a dollar sign on the other. Anoint the carvings with the oil and visualize the money coming to you as you rub it in thoroughly.

3. Fold the paper and set it beneath the candleholder.

4. Light the candle and meditate on attaining your money goals while continuing to visualize it manifesting.

5. Allow the candle to burn completely. If needed, blow out the candle and relight it each consecutive day until it is completely gone. You'll soon see financial improvement.

RITUAL OF GRATITUDE

Express gratitude for the fortunes you have to ensure continued abundance. This simple bath spell to give thanks to the universe when things are going well for you will ensure you continue to receive its blessings.

MATERIALS

Shovel

White rose

Scissors

5 fallen branches

INSTRUCTIONS

1. Take your materials to a private space in nature where you will not be disturbed.

2. Look for 5 fallen branches or twigs and collect them along your way.

3. Dig a shallow hole once you've found the perfect spot.

4. Pick the petals from the rose one at a time and place them into the hole as you say what you are thankful for out loud—the good, bad, beautiful, and sad.

5. Use the scissors to cut a small lock of your hair and place it into the hole as a symbolic offering.

6. Cover your offering with soil and place the five twigs on top of it in the shape of a pentagram. Ground and center yourself. Relax into the environment and honor your gratitude for self-growth. Move forward knowing that all is as it should be, and more great things are on their way to you.

TRANSIT MAGIC FOR JUPITER

The chart below can be used to further enhance or develop your astrological magic with Jupiter. Use astrological software or apps to determine the current or future transits of Jupiter and create spells or rituals that correspond to the mundane themes outlined below.

HOUSE OR SIGN	MUNDANE THEMES	MAGICAL RECOMMENDATIONS
First or Aries	You exude happiness and joy during this time. Your creative ideas surge with energy.	Spells for physical energy and stamina are a good idea. Candle magic is perfect for success in goals.
Second or Taurus	Financial gain and improvements are possible. High risk equals high reward.	It's a perfect time to work spells for abundance and prosperity and to increase your connection to luxury.
Third or Gemini	Your interactions with others come more easily than ever.	It's a great time for spells involving forgiveness or mending bonds and repairing miscommunications.
Fourth or Cancer	Familial relations are easy now. Expansion of family or living situations is possible.	Perform spells involving relocation and magical "spring cleaning" by purging what no longer is useful and rearranging your home.
Fifth or Leo	Creativity expands during this period. If you are single, you will find an increased opportunity for dating.	It's a good time for creative magic—anything to assist in drawing inspiration to you for passionate goals. Also, it's a good time for fertility spells, as well as love spells to attract new lovers.
Sixth or Virgo	Routines expand. It's a good time for promotions and teambuilding at work. Health improvements come into focus.	This is a good time for self-healing. Create a witchy self-care regimen including daily devotions, meditation, etc.

HOUSE OR SIGN	MUNDANE THEMES	MAGICAL RECOMMENDATIONS
Seventh or Libra	Growth in partnership and love are on tap now.	Spells to increase the loving bond between you and others are advisable. It's an excellent time for spells for marriage and proposals. Witchy weddings to bless the couple are great.
Eighth or Scorpio	A heightened intuition will allow you to read others better now. Sexual increases may occur.	Carry labradorite with you to enhance your intuition. Spells for lust are a good idea. Practice sex magic.
Ninth or Sagittarius	Travel is favorable now. Expand your experience of the world and inspiration in it.	Travel to a witchy location such as Salem, New Orleans, or the Southwest deserts of the United States. Tap into the magic of the place for inspiration and growth.
Tenth or Capricorn	Careers expand. Promotions and recognition are possible. Public opportunity arises.	Spells for career improvement or changing jobs are advisable. If looking for work, create a power sigil to overlay as a watermark on your resume. Be sure that it is only at 1 percent to 5 percent visible so that it is unseen to the naked eye.
Eleventh or Aquarius	It's the perfect time to network and connect with the community. Friendship circles may increase.	Perform spells for blessing the community, including local businesses. Place crystals for attraction and protection outside of businesses, including pyrite and clear quartz.
Twelfth or Pisces	Spirituality comes into focus. Healing is necessary.	Use meditation techniques to explore your shadow self and begin healing your mind, body, and spirit. Burn white and purple candles during this time.

CHAPTER 11

SATURN: RESPONSIBILITY & RESILIENCE

In classical astrology, Saturn was considered the last planet because it was the most distant cosmic body that could be seen from Earth. Taking this into consideration, Saturn's primary function is to provide boundaries. It is the literal end of reality. Saturn placements in a natal chart showcase how an individual will learn from the world and face fears, establish boundaries, and be limited by them in life. It is also connected to legacy, order, rules, justice, and obligations. Call upon its energy to stop yourself from partaking in toxic situations and create justice and structure. The chapter that follows will explore using these Saturnian themes in astrological magic, including spells, rituals, and considerations for Saturn's transits.

SATURNIAN MEDITATION

This meditation is designed for you to tap into all things Venus—love, beauty, pleasure, and sensuality. Perform it on a Friday or during the hour of Venus.

MATERIALS

Bergamot tea

Laptop or smartphone
   (optional)

Cushion or yoga mat to sit on

Lighter/matches

Patchouli incense

Patchouli oil

Journal and pen

INSTRUCTIONS

1. Brew and pour yourself a cup of bergamot tea. Find a comfortable and silent place to relax.

2. Play the ASMR/white noise audio of Saturn sounds found in my public Planetary Magic Meditation playlist on YouTube (see Resources on page 174) to focus your meditation and amplify Saturn's energy.

3. Get into a comfortable and relaxed position. Light the incense and fan the smoke in your direction. Apply a small amount of oil to your wrists and clavicle.

4. Sip your tea and close your eyes. Breathe deeply through your nose for 10 seconds before slowly exhaling through your mouth.

continued

5. Visualize Saturn and reflect on the following: What are my limits? In what ways do I feel restricted? Do I set firm boundaries with others and situations? How can I better establish boundaries for my mental and energetic health? What are my obligations? What are my disciplines? In what ways have I evolved over the years? Am I still holding myself back? What justice has not yet been served? How can order be brought to the situation?

6. Remain in the meditative state for at least 30 minutes before you slowly come back to consciousness. Record any revelations in your journal.

AMULET AGAINST TOXICITY

This is a simple binding spell used to create a protection amulet. It is designed to shield you from toxic individuals and situations and establish firm boundaries.

MATERIALS

Black marker
Full-length photo of yourself
Black chime candle and holder
Obsidian crystal

String of ivy
Cypress oil
Lighter/matches
Black drawstring pouch

INSTRUCTIONS

1. Use the black marker to draw a thick circle around yourself in the photo.

2. Place the candle and its holder on top of the photo. Place the obsidian at the base. String the ivy along the drawn circle on the photo, encasing the candle inside.

3. Anoint the candle with cypress oil and light the wick saying, "Saturn, planet of limits and boundaries, help me to set restrictions on those people and situations that are toxic to me. Protect me. It is my will, so must it be."

4. Allow the candle to burn completely and cool down. Fold the photo and place it in the drawstring pouch with any candle remains, ivy, and obsidian. Seal it shut and dab a bit of cypress oil on your index finger and trace the symbol for Saturn onto the bag. Allow it to dry. Carry the bag with you to protect yourself around toxic individuals.

REVERSING NEGATIVITY SPELL

This is a spell to bring justice and order and banish negativity that is being sent your way.

Knife

Hand mirror

Black chime candle and holder

Lighter/matches

1. Use the knife to chip away at the base of the candle to expose the wick.

2. Carve the name of the individual or situation that is causing negativity for you on one side of the candle. You can even just carve the word "injustice" or "negativity." On the other side, carve the astrological glyph for Saturn.

3. Set the mirror flat on a level surface. Place the candle securely in its holder on top of the mirror. Be sure the candle itself is upside down so the newly exposed wick is visible.

4. Light the newly exposed wick, calling upon the universal forces of justice with these words: "I reverse the negativity sent to me. I deflect all ill-will cast unto me. May it be returned to the sender swiftly."

5. Allow the candle to burn completely out and discard any scraps.

6. Place the mirror in a windowsill so that the reflective side faces outside. You will be protected from negativity, as it will return to the sender.

UNBINDING RESTRICTION

Working with Saturn can help free you from fears, obstacles, and preconceived judgments that hold you back. This spell is a ritualistic release, meant to free you from whatever holds you back. It is best performed on the day and/or hour of Saturn.

MATERIALS

Black candle

Fireplace or firepit (If you have neither, you may use a cauldron/fireproof bowl, but use caution and fire safety.)

Black cord in the length of your height

INSTRUCTIONS

1. Place the black candle and cauldron or firepit in front of you.

2. Interweave the cord around both of your wrists, creating a slight binding.

3. Close your eyes and contemplate whatever you feel restricted by—fears, people, circumstances, etc. Begin to unravel the cord from your wrists and tie a knot in the cord for each restriction as you visualize it.

4. Place the knotted cord on the ground in front of you, outstretched horizontally. Step over the cord. Pick it up and set it on fire in the fireplace, pit, or cauldron, saying, "It's time to set myself free. I let go of everything that holds me back, everything that restricts me. By the power of my will and transformation of the flame—may I be free."

5. Watch the cord burn in totality while chanting: "I free my mind. I free my body. I free my spirit." Once the cord has burned, put out the fire and move forward in your freedom.

TRANSIT MAGIC FOR SATURN

The chart below can be used to further enhance or develop your astrological magic with Saturn. This planet's transits last for about three years. You can use astrological software or apps to determine the current or future transits of Saturn and create spells or rituals that correspond to the themes outlined below. Saturn influences responsibility and limitations, so these will be key themes during the transits.

HOUSE OR SIGN	MUNDANE THEMES	MAGICAL RECOMMENDATIONS
First or Aries	Spiritual and emotional growth and a need to share with others come into focus. You may feel constrained creatively. Ambition may feel off—or increased responsibility may come into play.	Spellcraft to maximize your energy and drive are advisable. Spells for confidence are great, especially when dealing with physical appearance. Enchant your outfits or jewelry. Wear power crystals and colors. Magic to increase creativity may balance blockages.
Second or Taurus	A strong desire to figure out your money situation is at play. Pay off debt and create a financial plan.	Create a budget, print it, and place it on your altar with a green candle. Carve the dollar symbol into wax and Saturn's glyph. Light the candle regularly to help anchor your financial responsibility.
Third or Gemini	You will have a desire to express yourself with intellect and depth. It's a good time for writing. Be mindful of your communication. Careless words might come back to haunt you. Be careful signing contracts.	Keep a journal of affirmations to keep your mental focus on track. Use mirror magic and speak the affirmation out loud as you get ready for the day.

HOUSE OR SIGN	MUNDANE THEMES	MAGICAL RECOMMENDATIONS
Fourth or Cancer	You may feel a greater sense of responsibility on the home front. You may have to take care of family members or consider a home purchase.	Perform house blessings. Burn incense or smudge wands with rose petals. Use Florida water or rose water to wash floors and surfaces. Anchor the foundation of your home with rose quartz or amethyst crystals.
Fifth or Leo	Boundaries and responsibility are connected to your pleasures in life. Romances may fizzle out as boundaries are set or get more serious. There's a potential for children.	Magical efforts should be focused on happiness and preservation of all your favorite pleasures. Focus on practices that bring you the most happiness and make you feel your most magical.
Sixth or Virgo	More responsibility in your daily routine is on tap. Work demands increase. Time to get serious about your health, particularly mental health and the impact of stress.	Come up with a magical self-care routine to recharge your mind, body, and spirit during this time.
Seventh or Libra	Increased responsibility or limitations in partnerships—both business and romantic—make an appearance. It can be a good time for new business opportunities or romances or be a period of stagnation.	Magic involving harmony will offset any frustrations in partnerships. Be mindful that additional care will need to be established. Spells to increase compassion, compromise, and strengthening of bonds are advisable.
Eighth or Scorpio	Sexual desire may be low. Interest in the occult and supernatural may peak. Joint financial opportunities may present themselves; be mindful and don't go into them naively.	Magic connected to all levels of intimacy will be beneficial. Sex magic to manifest your desires is perfect now. Spend time developing your intuitive nature with divination tools such as tarot, oracle, scrying, tea leaf reading, or any other oracular art.

→

HOUSE OR SIGN	MUNDANE THEMES	MAGICAL RECOMMENDATIONS
Ninth or Sagittarius	Intellectual responsibility may increase. This is a good time to expand on your education and learn new things. Remain open-minded to other philosophies and ways of life. Restrict travel.	Spells for wisdom and direction will help you fulfill the increased desire for education. Minimize friction with travel by making your home a magical sanctuary that you do not wish to leave. Brush up on literature and research occult philosophy.
Tenth or Capricorn	Saturn is at home here. This brings advances on the career front. Hard work will bring big rewards. However, if you do not take career responsibilities seriously, you will find limitations.	Any magical efforts toward your career are advisable now, as are spells to increase financial prosperity. Think about your goals and legacy and anchor them with your witchcrafting. Work with oranges, greens, golds, and silvers. Tiger's eye and carnelian will strengthen ambition.
Eleventh or Aquarius	Increased responsibilities in community and group efforts come into focus. Friendships can strengthen and grow or fall apart.	Now is a good time to work on creating harmony in your circle of friends and community. It is the perfect time to do spells to attract new friends or strengthen established bonds.
Twelfth or Pisces	This is a period of transition and spiritual growth and a time for the rebirth of your ideas and individuality. Spiritual responsibility comes into play.	Now is the time to turn inward and focus on developing your spirituality. Take up regular meditation or yoga. Reflect on your growth and what has held you back. Strive to push past that during this time.

CHAPTER 12

URANUS: COMMUNITY & REBELLION

Uranus is the first of the outer planets, which all represent aspects of the collective unconsciousness. Called the "Great Awakener," Uranus challenges us to step beyond the restrictions placed by Saturn and move into a place of freedom. It is a planet of progress and rebellion. It is also connected to acts of humanitarianism and necessary revolution. Uranus placements in a natal chart showcase how and when someone may take risks or rise to the occasion when confronted by unexpected change. It also has to do with your relationship to community. This chapter focuses on using the energy of Uranus in spells and rituals. It includes an overview of themes to consider with Uranus's transits so that you can make the most of your astrological spellcraft!

URANIAN MEDITATION

The following meditation is designed for you to tap into Uranus's powers of rebellion and community.

MATERIALS

Chamomile tea

Laptop or smartphone
(optional)

Cushion or yoga mat to sit on

Neroli incense

Lighter/matches

Neroli oil

Journal and pen

INSTRUCTIONS

1. Make a cup of chamomile tea and bring it to a comfortable and quiet place.

2. Play the ASMR/white noise audio of the planet's sounds found in my public Planetary Magic Meditation playlist on YouTube (see Resources on page 174) to help focus your meditation and call in Uranus's energy.

3. Take a seat in a relaxed stance. Light the incense and fan the smoke in your direction. Apply a dab of oil to your wrists and clavicle.

4. Close your eyes and breathe deeply through your nose for 10 seconds before slowly exhaling through your mouth.

5. Visualize the planet Uranus as you reflect on the following: In what ways can I better express my individuality? In what ways do I rebel from society's expectations? How invested am I in the community? What is my role in social situations (i.e., am I a planner, leader, etc.)? What humanitarian interests do I have? How do I use technology to connect with others?

6. Remain in the meditative state for at least 30 minutes before you slowly come back to consciousness. Record any revelations in your journal.

COMMUNITY BLESSING SPELL

Uranus's energy is connected to humanitarianism and aiding the community. This spell acts as a blessing of good fortune to those in your neighborhood.

MATERIALS

Knife

White candle

Silver or gold mica

Handful of coins

A variety of freshly cut flowers

Lighter/matches

INSTRUCTIONS

1. Use the knife to carve the name of your town into the white candle. Add a bit of mica to the carving and place the candle in the center of your altar.

2. Create a circle around the candle with the coins and flowers, representing beauty, attraction, and abundance.

3. Light the candle and say: "By the power of Uranus, I ask that this community be blessed with good fortune for all."

4. Continue to burn the candle a little each day until it is completely gone. Take any wax remains, coins, and flowers and sprinkle them around the neighborhood to attract blessings to your community.

SOCIAL MEDIA WITCHERY

Not only is Uranus connected to the community, but also to advancements in technology. Therefore, social media is in Uranus's field of influence. This simple spell uses Uranus to help bless your social media presence and build a community of support.

MATERIALS

Pen and paper   Internet access
Smartphone or laptop

INSTRUCTIONS

1. Determine what your social media post will be about. Ask yourself if it needs to be said, if it is of service to the community, and if it celebrates your personal magic.

2. Create a sigil that personifies what you wish to share. Make a mantra. It could be something as simple as "I bless you with happiness."

3. Write your mantra on the piece of paper.

4. Cross out all the vowels of the sentence. In my example, this becomes "BLSSWTHHPPNSS."

5. Remove all duplicate letters. The example becomes "BLSWTHPN."

6. Sketch a symbol that combines all the letters remaining. Have fun and be creative.

7. Take a photo of your sigil.

8. Use the photo-editing software of your choice to overlay the symbol on whatever photo you plan to post on your profile. Lower the opacity of the sigil to 1 percent so that it is essentially invisible to the naked eye.

9. Share your post on your social accounts. Repeat this process whenever you have a magical message to share on the witch web.

SPELL FOR LIBERATION

Society can be very toxic when it comes to how people are allowed to express individuality. This spell will help you push beyond the constructs of society.

MATERIALS

Several strips of paper

Pen

Small glass jar

Paper bag

Hammer

INSTRUCTIONS

1. Think about the ways in which you rebel. On each strip of paper, write a key characteristic that makes you stand out from others.

2. Add a bit of saliva to each piece of paper to tie it to your energy.

3. Place the strips of paper in the small glass jar.

4. Set the jar in the brown paper bag and roll the opening down so that the glass is secure within the bag.

5. Reflect upon all the words in the jar. Feel what they represent vibrating through you. Say: "I free the unique qualities in me smashing expectations and confines. So mote it be!"

6. Use the hammer to smash the jar inside the bag. As you do so, feel yourself breaking free from society's confines so that your unique individuality can be freely expressed.

7. Unroll the bag carefully and discard the broken pieces. As you do, say: "I am free."

TRANSIT MAGIC FOR URANUS

The table below can be used to further enhance or develop your astrological magic with Uranus. This planet takes about seven years to fully transit through a house/sign. Being that this planet influences freedom and individuality, these will be key themes. Use astrological software or apps to determine the current or future transits of Uranus and create spells or rituals that correspond to the themes outlined below.

HOUSE OR SIGN	MUNDANE THEMES	MAGICAL RECOMMENDATIONS
First or Aries	This is a powerful time to express yourself and rebel against society's expectations of your physical appearance.	Enchant your wardrobe, jewelry, and beauty products. Experiment and play with appearance. Express yourself magically.
Second or Taurus	Rebellion of finances and security will create instability. Save now for unexpected expenses.	This is a good period to work on protecting your finances. Infuse blessings and protection into your money magic. Use pyrite to attract prosperity and protection.
Third or Gemini	Interest in technology will arise. Your imagination and creativity will expand and break boundaries. Unexpected travel can occur.	Keep crystals from the quartz family near your electronics to help conduct energy. Tap into techno-witchery by creating electronic sigils. Start a blog or new social media account to share information and ideas.
Fourth or Cancer	Unexpected and unstable connections to your home are the theme now. You may experience the sudden need to relocate. It's a good time to renovate or redecorate for security and comfort.	Any magical effort associated with changing your homelife to increase comfort is recommended. If you are looking to move, spells to facilitate this are beneficial now.

$\longrightarrow$

HOUSE OR SIGN	MUNDANE THEMES	MAGICAL RECOMMENDATIONS
Fifth or Leo	It's a good period to expand on your pleasures. Creative arts will pay off. New and unexpected romances can occur.	Perform magic associated with creativity and passion. Reds, pinks, and oranges are good colors to use in your magic. Attraction and love are advisable now.
Sixth or Virgo	New ideas at work can lead to unexpected challenges. Fad diets or exercise regimens are likely now. Alternative medicines may be on your radar.	Magic associated with your physical health is a good idea. Do regular healings and cleansings. Bath magic is a great way to incorporate relaxation into your practice.
Seventh or Libra	Breakups and divorces are likely, as partners feel a need for more individuality. Old flames can come back into the picture. Business partnerships may end.	Focus on self-love. This will help offset any painful transitions in relationships. Work with affirmations, mirror magic, rose quartz, and keep pink or white roses in your space.
Eighth or Scorpio	Sexuality will feel unique and exploratory. Newfound interest in fetishes and taboos is possible. Joint finances may become unstable.	Spells and magic connected to sexual liberation will be empowered by the universe now.
Ninth or Sagittarius	Alternative spiritual and philosophical interests will peak. Travel plans will be unpredictable.	Take this time to explore your spirituality. Read books on different philosophies and ways of life. Incorporate what works into your path. Take yourself out of your comfort zone.
Tenth or Capricorn	Career stress is likely. Unexpected changes may occur at work. A sudden promotion or job loss is possible.	Think about professional goals, and use magic to achieve them. Blessings for career luck are advisable, as are protection spells for job security and fortune.

HOUSE OR SIGN	MUNDANE THEMES	MAGICAL RECOMMENDATIONS
Eleventh or Aquarius	A lot of social networking will occur. New friendships will help develop interests in how to better serve communities. Service in some capacity will occur.	Anchor your magic in being of service to others. If you wish to manifest something for your own personal gains, do so in a way that will benefit others. For example, if you cast a spell for prosperity, do it so that you can then use that money to help others in some capacity. Use a love spell to bring comfort and compassion to another.
Twelfth or Pisces	Unexpected secrets may be revealed, showing who truly has your best interests at heart. Your intuition will be in overdrive, and skepticism about others' intentions may surface.	Magical efforts should be focused on truth. Identify what your truth is and how you can share that with others. The more you speak and show your truth to the world, the more you will inspire others to do the same. Also, spells to heighten your intuition will be helpful during this time.

CHAPTER 13

NEPTUNE: IMAGINATION & SPIRITUALITY

Neptune is a dreamy planet linked to spirituality and the subconscious mind. It is deeply connected to the magic of you and how you find hope. Neptune placements illuminate fantasies—everything from dreams, hopes, and fears to harmful illusions. This planet is sometimes seen as one of escapism and can showcase vices used to escape from reality. Use Neptune's energy to reflect on yourself and surrender control in favor of self-care to realign your mind, body, and spirit. This chapter focuses on using these themes magically as we explore Neptune's energy. Included are a handful of spells and rituals inspired by Neptune's energy, along with an overview of themes for the planet's transits.

NEPTUNIAN MEDITATION

The following meditation is designed to help you tap into Neptune's powers of imagination and spirituality.

MATERIALS

Lavender tea

Laptop or smartphone
(optional)

Cushion or yoga mat to sit on

Lavender incense

Lighter/matches

Lavender oil

Journal and pen

INSTRUCTIONS

1. Make a cup of lavender tea and bring it to a comfortable and silent place.

2. Play the ASMR/white noise audio of Neptune's sounds found in my public Planetary Magic Meditation playlist on YouTube (see Resources on page 174) to focus your meditation and call in Neptune's energy.

3. Sit in a relaxed stance. Light the incense and fan the smoke in your direction. Apply a dab of oil to your wrists and clavicle.

4. Close your eyes and breathe deeply through your nose for 10 seconds before slowly exhaling through your mouth.

5. Visualize the planet Neptune as you reflect on the following: Where am I in my spirituality at this moment? What are my spiritual morals and ethics? How do I use my imagination in reality? Are there any reoccurring themes in my dreams? How do I feel about them? What do I need to escape from? In what ways do I seek escape? In what ways am I compassionate? How can I be more self-compassionate?

6. Remain in the meditative state for at least 30 minutes before you slowly come back to consciousness. Record any revelations in your journal.

PROPHETIC DREAM PILLOW

Neptune is associated with the imaginative dreamworlds and intuition. Here, you will create a dream pillow to enhance prophetic dreams.

MATERIALS

2 pieces blue silk fabric cut in 6-inch squares

Needle and thread

1 handful dried chamomile

1 handful dried lavender

Tumbled piece labradorite

7 drops blue chamomile essential oil

Journal and pen

INSTRUCTIONS

1. Position the two pieces of silk fabric so that the outside sections are back to back.

2. Use the needle and thread to stitch three of the four sides together. Turn the resulting pocket of fabric inside out.

3. Fill the pillow with dried herbs and the crystal.

4. Stitch the open side of the pillow closed by folding the raw edges of the cloth inward.

5. Enchant the pillow before bed by applying the seven drops of blue chamomile essential oil to the fabric. State: "As I rest my head, here in this bed, may I see the prophecies that are meant for me."

6. Place the pillow under your head. Drift off to a peaceful slumber.

7. Record any visions in your journal come morning.

PAINTING MAGIC

Fluid paintings are a fun and imaginative way to connect with Neptune's artistic energies to help enhance your imagination and visualize your magical goals.

MATERIALS

Newspapers, magazines, or plastic tablecloth

Dish soap

Water

Multiple plastic cups depending on number of colors you are using

Acrylic paint in as many or as few colors as you'd like

Mixing sticks

Canvas of your desired size

Spray lacquer/sealant (optional)

INSTRUCTIONS

1. Refer to page 69 to select a variety of colors that connect to your magical goal.

2. Lay down newspapers, magazines, or plastic on a level table to protect your space and for ease of cleanup.

3. Combine a small amount of dish soap and water in one plastic cup.

4. Fill the remaining cups with acrylic paint, one per color. Mix a small amount of the water and soap solution in each paint cup until the consistency is runny.

5. Begin layering several colors of paint in a separate plastic cup.

6. Place your canvas on your covered table and place the cup of layered paint open-side down on the canvas. Tap the bottom of the cup before lifting it to get as much color out as possible.

continued

7. Move the canvas around so the paint covers every inch and drips off the sides. Continue this process until the mixing paint creates desirable shapes or patterns, all while focusing intently on the mixing colors and visualizing your goals.

8. Lay the canvas down flat and allow it to dry for at least a full day. Apply a sealant if you wish once the paint has dried and hang the painting near your altar or in a space you regularly see.

WATERS OF NEPTUNE BATH POTION

Whenever you are looking for a little "leveling up" of your spiritual practice, make this spiritual potion for spiritual awakening and add it to a warm bath.

MATERIALS

2 parts carrier oil (fractionated coconut or jojoba)

2 parts blue lotus essential oil

1 part neroli essential oil

1 part myrrh essential oil

1-oz. bottle

1 small tumbled larimar or aquamarine crystal

Pinch light blue mica

Knife

White or light blue candle

Lighter/matches

INSTRUCTIONS

1. Combine the carrier, blue lotus, neroli, and myrrh oil in the glass bottle.

2. Add the tumbled crystal to the bottle, along with a pinch of light blue mica.

3. Cap and shake the mixture vigorously and chant for Neptune's assistance: "I call upon the powers of Neptune to enchant thee. Awaken and empower spirituality in me."

4. Use the knife to carve the glyph for Neptune into the candle. Anoint it with the newly mixed oil. If you wish, rub more mica onto the candle to give a more dreamy, shimmering effect.

5. Draw a warm bath. Add seven drops of the oil to the bath.

6. Dim the lights and light the candle, and place it on one of the tub's corners.

7. Enter the bath. Soak in the water for 20 minutes. As you do, focus on your spirituality and allow the waters of Neptune to saturate your mind, body, and soul.

8. Rinse, dry off, and repeat as needed.

TRANSIT MAGIC FOR NEPTUNE

Neptune can spend close to 14 years transiting a sign or house. Spirituality and dreams are highlighted during this time. Use astrological software or apps to determine the current or future transits of Neptune and create spells or rituals that correspond to the themes outlined below.

HOUSE OR SIGN	MUNDANE THEMES	MAGICAL RECOMMENDATIONS
First or Aries	Your identity and ambitions will become saturated with spirituality. You will come off as mystical and enchanted.	Dress and physically express yourself with spirituality. Wear crystals to empower your personal magic.
Second or Taurus	Spiritual luxury is at hand. Your relationship with money may change at this time as you break through the illusions of finance.	Examine your relationship with material items. Use magic to feel secure and happy without physical security blankets. Anchor your practice with deep reflection and meditation.
Third or Gemini	Spiritual communication will be at play. Your imagination will be in overdrive with dreamy surrealism.	Be creative with your magic. Write stories, blogs, or poems or work on your Book of Shadows.
Fourth or Cancer	Your home will become a spiritual sanctuary to which you retreat for rest and rejuvenation.	Perform regular house blessings. Use incense, crystal grids, and candles to empower your home with energy. Make spiritual artwork. Incorporate feng shui into your magical practice.
Fifth or Leo	Your creative expression will be tapped into spiritualism or heightened imagination.	Anchor your happiness in spiritual exploration. Daydream and use magic to turn all desires into manifestations. Now is a perfect time to go after anything you wish.

HOUSE OR SIGN	MUNDANE THEMES	MAGICAL RECOMMENDATIONS
Sixth or Virgo	A collision of spirituality and health take center stage.	Alternative healing approaches such as acupuncture, Reiki, and crystal medicine will be good to explore and integrate into your practice now.
Seventh or Libra	A period of illusion in partnerships is at hand. You may experience codependency and attachment. Alternatively, fantasy over "perfection" in partners can lead to disappointment.	Self-love spells will ease codependent tendencies. Allow your spirituality to become your partner and nourish it as you would another. Spells and rituals for harmony and balance are a good idea.
Eighth or Scorpio	Intuition and psychic connections can increasingly grow during this time. Your thoughts may become focused on death and what you leave behind.	It's a great time to become more knowledgeable about reincarnation and past lives. Any magical efforts to strengthen intuition and psychic ability will do well now.
Ninth or Sagittarius	You will become a spiritual seeker. Dust off the passport, as significant travel is expected.	If you have strong desires to travel to specific locations, use prosperity spells for finances to travel. If you do not know where to go, ask the universe to guide you to where you will learn the most. You may be surprised at how close to home you are taken.
Tenth or Capricorn	Others will begin to take notice of you. They may be attracted or repelled by what you expose publicly. Be mindful of your image. Show compassion.	It's a good period to work glamour magic. Determine how you wish to be seen in the world and show it off with magical aesthetic. Bless images of you online by making watermarks.

→

HOUSE OR SIGN	MUNDANE THEMES	MAGICAL RECOMMENDATIONS
Eleventh or Aquarius	You are likely to attract creative and imaginative souls during this transit. Likewise, you may also attract individuals with codependency to drugs and alcohol. You may become hungry for spiritual community; be mindful not to fall into cult traps.	Casting spells for new friendships will pay off. Additionally, spells that assert your mental boundaries will weed out those who do not have your best interests at heart. Focus on how to be of service to the community and give back with your magical practice.
Twelfth or Pisces	An extended period of rest is possible. You may shut off from others and responsibilities to reconfigure your mind, body, and spirit. Now is a time for spiritual rebirth.	Sleep and dream spells will be powerful. Begin keeping a dream journal and record your memories upon waking. Watch for signs and symbolism in the mundane world.

CHAPTER 14

PLUTO: SACRIFICE & REBIRTH

Pluto is a dwarf planet found in the ring of celestial bodies beyond the orbit of Neptune. This cold, dark planet is named after the Roman god of the underworld. It is associated with the transformative themes of death and rebirth and with aspects of the hidden. As the most distant planetary body in our solar system, it is connected to larger groups and generations of people. It is often also associated with intimacy and the important things we share with others. Pluto placements indicate how one will react to secrets and intimacy and transform over time. This chapter explores using these Plutonian themes in astrological magic, including spells and rituals and considerations for Pluto's generational transits.

PLUTONIAN MEDITATION

The following meditation will help you tap into Pluto's powers of transformation, rebirth, and truth.

MATERIALS

Pomegranate tea

Laptop or smartphone
   (optional)

Cushion or yoga mat to sit on

Lighter/matches

Patchouli incense

Pomegranate oil

Journal and pen

INSTRUCTIONS

1. Make a cup of pomegranate tea and bring it to a comfortable and quiet place.

2. Play the ASMR/white noise audio of planetary sounds found in my public Planetary Magic Meditation playlist on YouTube (see Resources on page 174) to focus your meditation and call in Pluto's energy.

3. Sit in a relaxed stance. Light the incense and fan the smoke in your direction. Apply a dab of oil to your wrists and clavicle.

4. Close your eyes and breathe deeply through your nose for 10 seconds before slowly exhaling through your mouth.

5. Visualize the planet Pluto as you reflect on the following: What is my relationship to death? Is it something I fear? Why? How can I surrender my ego? In what ways will this affect my life? What can I purge, exorcise, or release currently? What have I hidden or suppressed? How can I expose and celebrate those things? What do I find taboo or fetishize? How does this release creativity?

6. Remain in the meditative state for at least 30 minutes before you slowly come back to consciousness. Record any revelations in your journal.

TO EXPOSE THE TRUTH

One of Pluto's greatest powers is digging deep to get to the truth of things. This spell calls upon this energy to help expose the truth of any situation you need clarity on.

Clay pot for planting
Potting soil
Lighter/matches
2 sticks amber incense for
  clarity

Knife
1 dark blue or indigo chime
  candle
Wormwood oil
White rose

INSTRUCTIONS

1. Fill the clay pot with the soil. Pat the soil in to ensure it is compact.

2. Light each incense stick and push them into the soil near the brim of the pot so they are parallel in position.

3. Dig a hole in the center of the soil. As you do this, chant: "I dig below the surface to reveal what is hidden."

4. Carve "TRUTH" on one side of the candle. Carve the word that identifies the truth you seek on the other (e.g., the name of the individual or institution you want the truth from or about).

5. Anoint the carvings with the wormwood oil. Place them into the soil and light it while saying: "That which is hidden is now exposed; from this may only truth be told."

6. Allow the candle to burn to completion. Stick the stem of the white rose into the center of the pot. Say: "With purity and grace, may truth and honesty now find their place."

7. The truth will reveal itself once the rose shrivels and dies.

HANGED MAN TAROT SPREAD

In the tarot, the Hanged Man represents the 12th card in the Major Arcana. Typically this card suggests the need for surrender and personal sacrifice—freely giving up something of importance to grow. Sacrifice is a powerful tool to help welcome more abundance into your life. However, it can sometimes be tough to determine just what we need to sacrifice. Here is a tarot spread that will help provide clarity on what sacrifices you need to make at this time for your personal and spiritual development.

MATERIALS

Lighter/matches

Pomegranate incense

Black candles

Black tourmaline, labradorite, or moldavite crystals (optional)

Tarot deck

Journal and pen

INSTRUCTIONS

1. Light the pomegranate incense and black candles in your space. If you have them, black tourmaline, labradorite, or moldavite crystals can be worn or placed alongside the cards to further stimulate the psychic connection.

2. Placed the Hanged Man card from your deck in front of you. Close your eyes and shuffle the cards. As you do, ask Pluto to guide you and show you what currently needs to be surrendered.

3. Draw four cards and place them into the below spread around the Hanged Man. Record your findings in your journal.

- **Origin (1):** Where that which you need to sacrifice originated

- **Obstacle (2):** The conflict you are experiencing

- **Sacrifice (3):** What you need to let go of
- **Awakening (4):** The outcome, or what you gain from letting go

RITUAL OF REBIRTH

This ritualistic rebirth should be performed when you are ready to shed the past and begin the next chapter of your life, spiritually and emotionally.

MATERIALS

White or silver gel pen

Black paper

8 black candles

Camphor oil

Lighter/matches

Patchouli or myrrh incense

Mirror

Black bath bomb

White floral soap (jasmine, lavender, rose, or gardenia scent is best)

1 white candle

Neroli oil

Cauldron/fireproof bowl

Champagne or lemonade in stem glass

INSTRUCTIONS

1. Spend the day in a state of reflection. Think about who you are in this place and time. What is your spiritual truth and how have you grown? What has made you angry? What pains have you had to endure? What successes have you achieved? Write your responses down on the paper.

2. Anoint the eight black candles with camphor oil and place them around the tub. Light them and the incense.

3. Disrobe and draw a warm bath.

4. Look at yourself in a mirror and read your list aloud. Scream, cry, laugh, dance, or do whatever action makes you feel as though you are ritually purging and transforming your old self.

5. Add the bath bomb to the water and enter the tub. Continue to reflect on all that you wish to shed.

6. Soak for up to 30 minutes before draining the water. In this moment, begin to cleanse yourself with the white soap.

7. Rinse with fresh water and dry off.

8. Anoint the white candle with neroli oil. Light it and touch the corner of your paper to the flame. Place it into the cauldron to burn.

9. Raise a glass of champagne or lemonade to yourself and celebrate where you envision yourself going.

10. Head to bed, and in the morning, wake up knowing that you have started a new chapter of your life.

TRANSIT MAGIC FOR PLUTO

Pluto's transits last for between 12 and 30 years and reflect the energy associated with a generation of individuals. You can use astrological software or apps to determine the current or future transits of Pluto and create spells or rituals that correspond to the themes outlined below. Pluto influences truth, evolution, and power in all areas of life, so these will be key themes during the transits.

HOUSE OR SIGN	MUNDANE THEMES	MAGICAL RECOMMENDATIONS
First or Aries	This is a period to focus on not allowing others to have power over you. Constant evolution occurs during this time.	It's a great time to anchor your magic in self-empowerment. Focus on your identity and how you want the world to see you. Work magic that boosts confidence to minimize victimhood and sabotage.
Second or Taurus	Loss of security is a common theme. It may feel as though nothing "good" ever stays for too long. You will gain understanding of possessions and what you truly need to be happy.	Take your magic inward and focus on your spirituality as an abstract influence and security. Actively work on a "less is more" attitude. Practice magic with minimal supplies and tools to heighten your magical self-worth.
Third or Gemini	Your mind and words have great power and influence over others. Use your mental power to your advantage during this transit.	Use magic to increase your personal power while also being beneficial to others. The more your influence is anchored in service, the more it will shift from "power over others" to "personal empowerment."

HOUSE OR SIGN	MUNDANE THEMES	MAGICAL RECOMMENDATIONS
Fourth or Cancer	Continuous transformation of family and home occur. Unexpected deaths or catastrophes may keep you from settling in one area. Familial secrets may come to light.	Become a magical nomad. Focus less on putting down roots and more on the spiritual lessons on your magical journey. Spells and rituals to amplify open-mindedness are advisable. Divination practices can help enhance intuitive nature.
Fifth or Leo	A deep and passionate love can transform your entire being. Jealousy is likely, and usually extreme. Hobbies can become a priority. Creative efforts can pay off.	Open your heart and express your love openly and willingly. The more you become a giving lover, the easier this transformative transit will be. This will enhance your relationships, attractiveness, and creative potentials.
Sixth or Virgo	Transformation of physical health will be an ongoing process. Your professional life will also undergo an intense transformation. Changing fields is likely.	Now is the perfect time to focus on your goals and plant the seeds of your intentions. Spells of patience will work well. Spells for harmony will ease tensions. Be sure to take time out to rejuvenate your mind, body, and spirit.
Seventh or Libra	All partnerships will experience power struggles and continued changes. Disharmony is likely, as is jealousy and lack of trust.	Work on curtailing jealousy. Reflect on what you have and not so much on what you don't. Rituals of gratitude (even for obstacles as a form of transformative growth) will help pull in more possibilities your way.

⟶

HOUSE OR SIGN	MUNDANE THEMES	MAGICAL RECOMMENDATIONS
Eighth or Scorpio	This is a powerful time for transformation. Sexuality will become intensified in your life and society. Taboo interests will be highlighted and explored.	Pluto is at home here. Explore sexuality magically. Sex magic or spells to awaken aspects of your sexuality will succeed.
Ninth or Sagittarius	As your beliefs change, you will also be interested in sharing and changing the beliefs of others. Watch out for dogma. Deep interests in psychology, research, sexuality, and death are possible.	Become a spiritual teacher or adviser. Work on continued education of a spiritual and magical nature, with the focus on teaching what you have learned. Express what works for you and how you practice as a suggestion rather than a fact.
Tenth or Capricorn	Ambition regarding career and legacy kicks into overdrive. A strong desire for control can make people and situations come off as tyrannical. Your career itself will undergo transformation. Go with the flow.	Research other career fields and do magic to enhance and amplify transferrable skills. Even if you are satisfied in your career, spells and rituals to enhance or change jobs will have favorable outcomes.
Eleventh or Aquarius	A deep obsession with causes of all kinds takes root. You will wish to help change and improve others' lives. Charity is important. Friendships are taken more seriously. A transformation of individuality and in how you contribute to society is possible.	Start a coven or magical group. Focus the magic that you all make on being of service to the community. It is important to ensure you have the same goals and outlook to avoid frustration and power struggles.
Twelfth or Pisces	A transformation related to psychological and unresolved issues awaits. Mental health becomes intertwined with spirituality. Spiritual truths give way for transformation. It's a time of rebirth.	Keep a spiritual journal to reflect on your progress. Each year, take a moment to review the outcomes of the year and see where you have grown. Burn petitions to tap into the transformative power of fire.

A FINAL WORD

You have reached the end of your magical exploration of the cosmos, at least for now. While you have explored a great deal of astrological concepts in this book, remember that this is just the beginning. This book is not meant to be a complete text for all things astrological. Continue to research and learn as much as possible and apply your newfound knowledge with practice. Remember to go at a pace that is best for you—there is no need to rush.

As you move forward in your astrological pursuits with magic, explore other points outside of the planets, such as the asteroids—which we did not have time to explore here. Also, continue studying other avenues of new age and occult practices to further enhance your magic. By doing so, you'll be able to further connect the dots and see how everything is truly intertwined in a universal web of witchery. Also, use the spells and rituals prescribed here as influencers for creating your own spells and rituals that fit your personal needs.

With that said, thank you for allowing me to be your tour guide of the cosmos. I hope that you have found something in this book that is useful on your path. Look to the stars every chance you get, and remember that they are also watching you and your magic. So, shine bright and go forth on your continued magical journey!

Blessed be,

Michael

The Glam Witch
xo

RESOURCES

Following is a list of recommended books, online resources, podcasts, and stores to continue your exploration of witchcraft and moon magic.

BOOKS

The Art Cosmic by Levi Rowland
This is an amazing and well-researched book that examines the seven classical planets of astrology with superb depth that is anchored in ceremonial magic.

Astrology for Real Life by Theresa Reed
This is a hip and modern guide to exploring all aspects of astrology. It is a thorough and wonderful companion book that could be used to further accentuate this book's teachings.

The GLAM Witch by Michael Herkes
My first book goes into great detail on the mythology and worship of Lilith, including how to use her astrologically to heal the shadow self.

Love Spells for the Modern Witch by Michael Herkes
Another book of mine, this one provides a detailed overview on astrological compatibility.

Planetary Spells & Rituals by Raven Digitalis
This is one of my favorite books on the magic of the cosmos. It provides a deeper look at astrological magic and ways to incorporate it into your practice.

ONLINE RESOURCES

Astro.com provides horoscopes, charts, calculations, and articles to make navigating your life in harmony with the cosmos easy.
Astro-Charts.com is an excellent resource for getting your natal chart.
Cafeastrology.com is another online hub for all things astrology related.
Planetary Magic Meditation Playlist (youtube.com/c/TheGlam WitchOfficial): I have created a public playlist on my YouTube channel for your convenience and recommend using it in various spells in part 2.

Witch Way Magazine (witch-way-magazine.myshopify.com) is a digital publication featuring curated articles about witch culture, craft, and daily life.

Witch With Me (WitchWithMe.com) is an online community for witches to further hone their craft.

PODCASTS

Fat Feminist Witch is a fun and sassy podcast that examines witchcraft and spirituality from a feminist perspective.

The Witch Daily Show is a daily podcast that goes over headlines, books, topics, witch-fails, and more.

The Witchcast Presented by Lucy Cavendish is a bewitching podcast for dreamers, misfits, seekers, and believers, hosted by internationally acclaimed witch Lucy Cavendish.

Witchin' & Bitchin' podcast is a thoroughly fun and modern sacred space for all witches to share their thoughts and ideas.

*Each listed podcast is available on multiple online channels, including iTunes and Spotify.

STORES

Bébé Vaudou (BebeVaudou.com) is owned by the immensely talented singer, songwriter, and witch Brooklynn and offers handcrafted candles and magical supplies.

Hex (HexWitch.com) is a wonderful shop to stock up on all your witchy necessities. It also hosts HexFest, an annual magical conference with presenters from around the world covering a wide array of topics for magical and spiritual practice.

REFERENCES

Cunningham, Scott. *Cunningham's Encyclopedia of Magical Herbs.* Woodbury, MN: Llewellyn Publications, 1985.

Digitalis, Raven. *Planetary Spells & Rituals: Practicing Dark & Light Magick Aligned with the Cosmic Bodies.* Woodbury, MN: Llewellyn Publications, 2010.

Edington, Louise. *The Complete Guide to Astrology: Understanding Yourself, Your Signs, and Your Birth Chart.* Oakland: Rockridge Press, 2020.

Herkes, Michael. *The GLAM Witch: A Magical Manifesto of Empowerment with the Great Lilithian Arcane Mysteries.* Dallas: Witch Way Publishing, 2019.

Herkes, Michael. *Love Spells for the Modern Witch: A Spell Book for Matters of the Heart.* Oakland: Rockridge Press, 2021.

Herkes, Michael. *Witchcraft for Daily Self-Care: Nourishing Rituals and Spells for a More Balanced Life.* Oakland: Rockridge Press, 2021.

Horne, Fiona. *Witch: A Magickal Journey.* London: Thorsons, 2000.

Leek, Sybil. *Sybil Leek's Astrological Guide to Successful Everyday Living.* New York: Random House, 1988.

Melody. *Love Is in the Earth: A Kaleidoscope of Crystals: The Reference Book Describing the Metaphysical Properties of the Mineral Kingdom.* Wheatridge, CO: Earth Love Pub House, 1995.

Reed, Theresa. *Astrology for Real Life: A Workbook for Beginners.* Newburyport, MA: Weiser Books, 2019.

Rowland, Levi. *The Art Cosmic: The Magic of Traditional Astrology.* New Orleans: Warlock Press, 2021.

Woolfolk, Joanna M. *The Only Astrology Book You'll Ever Need.* Lanham, MD: Taylor Trade Publishing, 2012.

INDEX

ACKNOWLEDGMENTS

Thank you to Callisto Media/Rockridge Press for another incredible writing opportunity, and specifically to Brian Sweeting for your assistance in editing this book.

To Megan Walsh for giving me my very first astrological reading, which set my love and appreciation for the cosmos into overdrive several years ago.

To Hudson Leick—the original Callisto—for the honor of reading my chart on my birthday in 2021 and sharing your intuitive wisdom with me.

Thank you to all my friends and family for your continued support, especially those who helped guide me in the writing of this book: Chris, Christina, Fiona, Gabe, Kay, Kiara, Lynne, Silvester, Tania, Theresa, Tonya, and Yazmin.

A big buzzing thank-you to Jerry, Lee, and the Buzzed by Zea family for your incredible support and the opportunity to make magic on a weekly basis at your wonderful salon!

And last but not least, thank YOU for picking up this book!

ABOUT THE AUTHOR

Michael Herkes (Chicago), also known as "the Glam Witch," has been a practicing modern witch for more than 20 years. He is a devotee of the goddess Lilith and focuses his practice on astrology, crystals, glamour, love, moon, and sex magic. Michael is the author of numerous books on witchcraft, including *The GLAM Witch*, *The Complete Book of Moon Spells*, *Witchcraft for Daily Self-Care*, *Love Spells for the Modern Witch*, and *Moon Spells for Beginners*, and has contributed articles and graphic design for *Witch Way Magazine*. A nationwide speaker, Michael has presented at festivals such as Gather the Witches, HexFest, and WitchCon, in addition to being featured in an exhibit on display at the Buckland Museum of Witchcraft in Cleveland, Ohio. Additionally, Michael offers astrological and tarot reading services through his website. To learn more and book an appointment, visit TheGlamWitch.com.